# TELL ME TO STAY

## CHARLOTTE BYRD

BYRD BOOKS, LLC

Identifiers

ISBN (e-book): 978-1-63225-056-8

ISBN (paperback): 978-1-63225-057-5

ISBN (hardcover): 978-1-63225-058-2

✽ Created with Vellum

## ABOUT TELL ME TO STAY

I am not a liar or a thief or a criminal. At least, not anymore. But here I am doing things that I promised myself I would never do again.

Nicholas Crawford made me an offer I couldn't refuse. He is dangerous and damaged but so am I. Our relationship is an addiction that we have to feed.

Now, things are about to get even more complicated.

Allegiances will be tested. Lies will be told. Truths will be revealed.

We have both made promises that we can't keep. The secrets we have uncovered only scratch the surface, and I'm afraid to find out what lies below.

All is not what it seems but I have to figure out the truth before it's too late.

*Decadent and delicious 3rd book of the new and addictive Tell Me series by bestselling author Charlotte Byrd.*

and that's how their story begins it's exhilarating with that nail biting suspense that keeps you riding on the edge the whole series. You'll love it!"

★★★★★

"What is Love Worth. This is a great epic ending to this series. Nicholas and Olive have a deep connection and the mystery surrounding the deaths of the people he is accused of murdering is to be read. Olive is one strong woman with deep convictions. The twists, angst, confusion is all put together to make this worthwhile read." ★★★★★

"Fast-paced romantic suspense filled with twists and turns, danger, betrayal, and so much more." ★★★★★

"Decadent, delicious, & dangerously addictive!" - Amazon Review ★★★★★

"Titillation so masterfully woven, no reader can resist its pull. A MUST-BUY!" - Bobbi Koe, Amazon Review ★★★★★

"Captivating!" - Crystal Jones, Amazon Review ★★★★★

"Sexy, secretive, pulsating chemistry..." - Mrs. K, Amazon Reviewer ★★★★★

"Charlotte Byrd is a brilliant writer. I've read loads and I've laughed and cried. She writes a balanced book with brilliant characters. Well done!" -Amazon Review ★★★★★

"Hot, steamy, and a great storyline." - Christine Reese ★★★★★

"My oh my....Charlotte has made me a fan for life." - JJ, Amazon Reviewer ★★★★★

"Wow. Just wow. Charlotte Byrd leaves me speechless and humble... It definitely kept me on the edge of my seat. Once you pick it up, you won't put it down." - Amazon Review ★★★★★

" Intrigue, lust, and great characters...what more could you ask for?!" - Dragonfly Lady ★★★★★

# WANT TO BE THE FIRST TO KNOW ABOUT MY UPCOMING SALES, NEW RELEASES AND EXCLUSIVE GIVEAWAYS?

Sign up for my newsletter: https://www.subscribepage.com/byrdVIPList

Join my Facebook Group: https://www.facebook.com/groups/276340079439433/

Bonus Points: Follow me on BookBub and Goodreads!

# ABOUT CHARLOTTE BYRD

Charlotte Byrd is the bestselling author of romantic suspense novels. She has sold over 1 Million books and has been translated into five languages.

She lives near Palm Springs, California with her husband, son, a toy Australian Shepherd and a Ragdoll cat. Charlotte is addicted to books and Netflix and she loves hot weather and crystal blue water.

Write her here:

charlotte@charlotte-byrd.com

Check out her books here:

www.charlotte-byrd.com

Connect with her here:

www.facebook.com/charlottebyrdbooks

www.instagram.com/charlottebyrdbooks

www.twitter.com/byrdauthor

Sign up for my newsletter: https://www.
subscribepage.com/byrdVIPList

Join my Facebook Group: https://www.
facebook.com/groups/276340079439433/

Bonus Points: Follow me on BookBub and
Goodreads!

facebook.com/charlottebyrdbooks

twitter.com/byrdauthor

instagram.com/charlottebyrdbooks

bookbub.com/profile/charlotte-byrd

All the Doubts

**Tell me Series**
Tell Me to Stop
Tell Me to Go
Tell Me to Stay
Tell Me to Run
Tell Me to Fight
Tell Me to Lie

**Wedlocked Trilogy**
Dangerous Engagement
Lethal Wedding
Fatal Wedding

**Tangled Series**
Tangled up in Ice
Tangled up in Pain
Tangled up in Lace
Tangled up in Hate
Tangled up in Love

**Black Series**
Black Edge
Black Rules
Black Bounds

## 1

## NICHOLAS
### WHEN I MEET WITH HIM...

The one thing you should know about me is that I'm a liar. I learned how to lie from my mother and lying was the only way I could survive growing up in that family.

Now, I lie for a living.

I wear a mask every day of my life. In my line of work, it's a prerequisite.

I was wearing a mask when I met Olive Kernes. I know what you want to hear.

You want me to say that I wanted to take it off as soon I as I had laid my eyes on her. You want me to say that I fell deeply in love with her and I could put the mask away.

But I'd be lying.

On occasion, I do tell the truth.

Olive came into my life as a result of yet another lie. Now, you're probably trying to figure out what part of what I told her is a lie.

Was my sister really her best friend growing up? Yes.

Is she really dead? Yes.

Did she write me a letter asking me to protect the one person who was ever there for her? Yes.

This was all true. So, what was the lie?

I paid off her debt because I need her.

Yes, I promised my dead sister that I would look out for her and I did. I took care of her debts and made her an offer she couldn't refuse.

I promised to pay her one million dollars to work with me for a year.

I made the offer partly to protect her because there's a bounty on her head. And partly, because I have a mission that I can't complete without her.

So, what's the lie?

I can't pay her. Not yet, anyway.

She thinks that the one million is set in stone but this stone is shattered and I need her help to put it back together.

It wasn't always a lie though. When I made the promise, I had the money.

It was tucked away safely in my bank account along with the other five million.

It's amazing how long six million can last if you invest it wisely. It can even grow to seven. But then *they* came along.

"I'll have what he's having," a man says to the bartender and sits down next to me, brushing up against my elbow.

His suit is a size too big and made of polyester. I wonder if he got it at a two for one deal at the same place he got that cheap haircut.

"Christ, what the hell is this?" He almost spits the drink out of his mouth.

"Water with ice," I say, looking at the bottles lining the shelves across from us.

"No, no, no," he says, shaking his head. "I'll have a glass of Macallan."

He is not off the clock so he's

technically not allowed to drink. He makes maybe seventy-thousand a year but that doesn't stop him from ordering a glass of whiskey that costs close to fifty dollars.

We both know that this is not a one-off occasion. He isn't celebrating anything. This is just a normal Tuesday.

"You know, I'm surprised to see you here, Nicky," Art Hedison says. No one has called me Nicky since I was eighteen but he says it every chance he gets. It's meant to put me in my place, but I refuse to let it.

"I don't know why," I say casually, taking a sip of my water. "You insisted that we meet."

The bartender hands him his glass. He swirls around the ice cubes for a moment before taking a swig.

"So, what are you doing back in Boston, Nicky?"

I don't know how much he knows. "I had some personal business."

Art turns to me.

His face contorts into a scowl. He thinks it's threatening.

It's not.

I know that only a year ago he was nothing more than a paper pusher and then he hit the jackpot by being assigned to my case.

This is the way he's going to grow up the ladder. I'm his ticket to a grand career at the Bureau.

"Don't forget who you are, Nicky. Or what we have on you," he says in his best bad cop impersonation.

Did he practice this in front of the mirror? I wonder.

"You are not to have any personal business while you are working for us."

He wants me to look at him, but I won't give him the satisfaction.

"Why did you want to meet, Art?" I ask.

"I prefer Mr. Hedison," he corrects me.

"I prefer Nicholas, so I guess we both should get used to disappointment."

Without another word, he gets out of

his seat and goes toward the back of the bar.

It's pretty empty, but it's still a public place and even he knows better than to discuss anything like this where anyone can hear us. Or maybe he's just going to use the john.

When I glance over at him, I see him waiting near the back door. He nods in my direction. I finish my drink and follow him outside.

"Took you long enough," he mumbles.

This isn't going as we had practiced.

Oh well, we can't all get what we want.

"I have a new job for you, Nicky," Art says after looking both ways down the long dirty alley. The nearest light is at the corner and it takes my eyes a few moments to adjust to the darkness.

"I thought your boss wasn't happy with my other job," I say.

"It's not my boss who wasn't happy, it was me," he corrects me, never missing an opportunity to massage his ego. I laugh to myself.

"My bad," I say with a tinge of sarcasm.

"Listen, don't forget who you are talking to," he says, taking a step closer to me. "I'm your only lifeline, you degenerate asshole."

I clench my jaw. Out of the corner of my eye, I see his hand reach for my collar but at the last moment he pulls it away.

It's technically illegal in the FBI to physically assault their independent contractors even if they are *unwilling* independent contractors.

"This is your last chance," Art says, waving his finger in my face. "If you fuck this up, the deal is off. We don't need you."

## 2

### NICHOLAS
#### WHEN I FIND OUT ABOUT MY NEW JOB...

I glare at Art. He and I both know it's a bluff. They do need me.

I'm their connection. I'm their way in. They may have an agent working their way up the ladder, but it's going to be a long time before anyone in the organization really trusts him. On the other hand, I'm one of their top people as far as independent contractors go.

"I thought that you would've been pleased that I delivered the laptop," I say. "Thought it would've at least brightened your mood a bit."

This catches Art by surprise. He has

been with the FBI for more than ten years
but he'd always worked a desk job.

He's still not very good at hiding his
hand. I get it, it takes a bit of practice to
lie as well as I do.

"What exactly should've pleased me?"
He finally asks after he gathers his
thoughts. "The part that the project came
in at three times the budget and took
three times as long. Or the part where
one of our valuable assets got killed and
got the local cops sniffing around?"

"Wait...what?" I ask, trying to process
what he had just said.

"Yeah, that's right." Art nods his head.
"You don't know everything, Nick. No
matter how much you think you do."

I knew that the job cost a lot more
than it should have and took a lot longer,
but what is this about a valuable asset?

"You thought that Caitlyn was just an
escort, right? Wrong. She worked for us
just like you are working for us. Under
the table, so to speak."

"Why?" I ask, taking a step back.

I didn't know her but I had researched

the escort agency that Dallas called. It's my job to know everything and I take my job very seriously.

I looked into everyone who worked there, women *and* men. I knew about their personal lives and their families. I knew their log-in information and what they liked to look at online. And nothing about her working for them came up.

"You are not the only one who is good at keeping secrets," Art says. "Occasionally, the FBI is, too."

I shake my head in disbelief. I know what they have on me but what did they have on *her*?

You see, that's the only way you get into this prestigious club.

They open a case on you, collect evidence, and then threaten to arrest you and send you to prison for years unless you can do something for them.

Take it from me, if you do illegal things, make sure you keep evidence of other people you work with who also do illegal things so you can use that as leverage and reduce your sentence.

I wasn't that smart so here I am.

I have to pay for my sins the hard way.

The problem with this job is that it's mandatory and it has no end date. Once I'm useless to them then they'll prosecute me for the crimes that they can prove.

Until then? I have to keep risking my life and limb in a series of impossible jobs that require me taking valuable things from very bad people. If I do it for long enough, I'm pretty certain that you will either find me in prison for the rest of my life or in a casket six feet under.

"Are you going to tell me what the job is or not?" I ask. "I don't have all day."

"No, you don't." Art laughs.

I furrow my brow.

He is acting way too cocky even for him.

"Owen Kernes. That name ring a bell?"

My throat closes up, but I tell myself to breathe. He may mean someone different. It's a pretty common name.

"Owen Kernes, your girlfriend's

brother who is getting out of prison as we speak," Art says, pulling out a cigarette.

With blood rushing between my temples, I can barely hear anything that he's saying. I watch as he puts the cigarette in between his teeth and lights it, taking a long drag.

"Quitting is a bitch, huh?" he says under his breath.

"I wouldn't know," I say. "I never smoked."

"Lucky bastard."

He takes a few puffs, exhaling each one right into my face. The smoke burns my eyes and tickles my throat but I don't give him the satisfaction of even one flinch.

"You couldn't have forgotten Owen, right? You had some history if I remember that correctly. What was it that happened again?" he asks. "Oh, that's right, you stole his girlfriend. You two were friends. That's cold, bro, really cold."

That's the gist but the details aren't there.

We weren't really friends.

And I went out with her first. When we hooked up, I had no idea that they were dating. But I don't think it's details like this that Art cares about.

"So, is that why he's my new job?" I ask. "Because we slept with the same girl?"

"Nope," Art says, popping a piece of gum in his mouth.

He chews it slowly and deliberately, making me wait.

"You were right," he says, blowing a bubble.

"About what?" I ask. He pops the bubble before answering.

"About all of the stuff you told Olive."

Blood drains away from my face.

My hands turn to ice.

He knows about her.

He knows what we talked about. How the *fuck* does he know that?

"Owen is getting out of prison because he made a deal. We had a little chat with the parole board and sped things up a few years."

I clench my fists but keep my face

stoic and under control. He can't see me sweat. He can't see me worry.

"The guys he testified against are after him. Or rather their bosses are. His old boss. Your old boss. They're also after your girlfriend."

"So...what?" I ask as nonchalantly as possible.

"Well, we need him and we need her. That's where you come in. That fight you had with her, that's over now. You are going to do everything in your power to make things nice with Owen. You get him to trust you. You get him to become your best friend."

"And then?" I ask.

"Then I'll be back with more instructions."

EARLIER THAT DAY...

## 3

## OLIVE
### WHEN I PICK HIM UP...

This should be a happy day but my stomach is in knots. Nicholas and I just had a huge fight and now I don't know where we stand. He is categorically against me going to pick up my brother from prison and I am categorically against this whole thing being any of his business.

Why does he have to be so impossible?

Why does he have to be so complicated?

Why does he have to be so difficult to get along with?

Why is this any of his business?

I'm so angry my knuckles are white from grasping the wheel too hard. I take a deep breath and force myself to release the hold just a little.

It's early morning and I have gotten no sleep. Nicholas and I argued well into the night and once I did get into bed my mind continued to race.

When my alarm went off at three in the morning, I was so awake that I didn't even need any coffee.

Breakfast was out of the question.

I couldn't force myself to eat a crumb but I did grab a power bar in case I got hungry later.

It's not going to be enough and I'm probably going to feast on junk food from the vending machines but at least my intentions are honorable.

"Fuck, Nicholas!" I yell, grabbing onto the wheel again while I slow down at a yellow light. The streets are deserted and soaked from the rain.

Don't you get it that I need you?

Don't you get it that you're being a selfish prick?

But, how could he? I ask myself. We had talked about Owen for hours but not once did I say what I really needed to say.

Even now, staring into the abyss of the dark street before me, I can barely admit it to myself.

I'm afraid.

I'm not so much afraid of Owen as I am afraid of seeing him again.

Writing is one thing. I can express almost anything through the written word.

But now that I actually have to see him in person? I'm terrified.

A million *'what-ifs'* rush through my mind.

What if he's not really the person who I imagined him to be?

What if we don't get along?

What if we have nothing to talk about?

What if he doesn't like me?

Don't you *fucking* get it, Nicholas? I need you here.

You could've been our *buffer*. You

could've been my protector in case...in case we had nothing to talk about.

But *you* had to make things complicated.

*You* had to put all of these things into my head about the person I have no choice but to pick up.

He's getting out on parole.

I'm his sister.

I'm the only person he has in the whole world.

I pull up next to the prison and park the car in the visitors' lot. I thought I had go through security again, but the guard at the gate tells me to just wait here.

"How long?" I ask.

"I have no idea, but it can take a while," he says.

I turn up the music to drown out Nicholas' words from my head but they just get louder.

"Owen gave evidence against some bad people and that's the only reason he's getting out on parole on his first try." I hear him say. "They are out for blood. They want revenge. They will get it from him and from anyone he cares about. There's a contract out on your head."

When I first found out that Nicholas' offer to spend the year with him was an elaborate protection plan, I was angry.

He had lied, and then he lied again.

But then we caught feelings.

At least, I did.

He said that he did, too, but what if that was just another lie?

Ever since we have been together two people have died.

Caitlyn, the escort, who interrupted my meeting with Dallas and the man who burst into my apartment and tried to kidnap me.

Caitlyn was an innocent and her blood is on both of our hands. She wouldn't be dead if I hadn't gone there behind Nicholas' back.

She wouldn't be dead if Nicholas hadn't called the agency when he thought I wasn't going to make it to the hotel room.

Caitlyn is dead because of our lies.

I feel guilty and full of regret and there's nothing I can do about it.

But what about the masked man?

Who was he and what did he really want?

Did he come because of Owen's testimony?

Or did he come because of Nicholas?

Nicholas' argument sounds plausible, but there are doubts that creep in around the edges.

The truth is that I don't really know anything about him.

I don't know anything about his past and I don't even really know anything about his present.

Whenever I feel like I'm on solid ground, I quickly discover that it's actually quicksand.

His life is a house of cards, one lie piling on another and another. And yet....

Yet, I'm drawn to him.

I want him. It's not *just* a sexual thing.

It's more of a physical thing.

I want to be in his presence. I want to

be with him. I want to know more
about him.

I want to know every secret and lie.

I want to know the truth even though
I am terrified.

But the thing that scares me the most
is *what if* I find out something that will
make it impossible for me to be
with him?

A loud knock on the window startles
me. It's a man with a shaved head and a
wide toothy smile.

"Owen!" I yelp, reaching for the
doorknob.

"No, stay there!" he yells, pointing to
the rain that is now falling sideways. "Just
let me in!"

He runs around the car as I unlock it.
I grab onto him before he even gets the
chance to close the door.

"It's so good to see you," he sobs into
my shoulder and tears start to flow down
my face.

# 4

## OLIVE
WHEN WE CATCH UP...

I t takes us a few minutes to finally pull away from each other. Our cheeks are wet and my throat has a big lump in the back of it.

Owen's eyes look bloodshot and his skin is sallow. His deep set eyes are adorned with thick dark lashes.

I reach over and wipe his eyes with my finger. He turns his face toward my open hand, kissing the bottom of my palm.

"It's so good to touch you, Olive," he says.

We have seen each other during my

visits but this is the first time in years that we have actually held each other.

When I had visited him in prison, we were allowed one rudimentary hug at the beginning and the end of each session and no touching the rest of the time.

"I know, I can't believe that you're actually here," I say, squeezing his shoulders in another embrace.

I run my fingers over the back of his head, feeling the prickles of his hair. I hope that he lets it grow out more now that he's out.

"Listen, let's get out of here," I say, turning on the engine.

"You've read my mind."

I drive back out onto the highway quickly and it's not until we are about ten miles out that a wave of relief starts to sweep over me.

Owen is actually free and no one came to get us in the parking lot.

Unsure as to what else to do to celebrate the occasion, I offer to take him out to a local diner.

Once inside, he orders a large

breakfast with three stacks of pancakes, two waffles, an omelet, and a refillable cup of black coffee. I opt for some avocado toast.

Driving over here, I thought that we would have nothing to talk about but the words come spilling out of both of us. We are practically speaking over each other.

Literacy is a big passion of his and he talks a lot about the fact that sixty percent of US inmates are functionally illiterate. They can understand some basic sentences but their reading and writing skills are basically at a seven year old's level, making it very difficult to get any meaningful employment.

I had no idea that Owen was dyslexic when he was a kid and our mom thought (and told him and everyone else) that he was just dumb.

In prison, he decided to get his high school diploma and his teacher discovered that he couldn't read. Once he learned, he consumed every book he could get his hands on and even started to work on a memoir about his life.

He spent the last few years of his incarceration teaching others to read and write.

I know all of this already from his emails and our conversations in the visitors' room, but it's wonderful to hear all of this again out in the free world. Whatever passion he conveyed earlier is only amplified out here.

"So, what about you? How's your career? How do you like your work?" he asks.

I take a deep breath.

The answer is not something that's going to make him happy. Should I lie or should we finally talk about the elephant in the room?

"It's fine. It's not my favorite thing and I don't really know if it's much of a career," I finally say, chickening out.

Owen tilts his head, biting feverishly into his waffle. "Tell me everything," he says, chewing with his mouth open.

"I don't really know where to start," I say, shrugging my shoulders. "It's just that you know that I worked my butt off to get into Wellesley. I majored in math, probably one of the hardest majors out there. I wanted to go to graduate school but I thought I would work first and save up some money. I don't know, I guess to get the feel of what it's like to be out there in the workforce."

"Yeah, go on," he urges me when I take a long pause to collect my thoughts.

This is the first time I have ever said any of this out loud and it feels foreign and completely unnatural. But I force myself to keep going.

"Well, it's not exactly all it's cracked up to be. Having a career, that is."

"What do you mean?" he asks.

"I don't know, but it doesn't really feel fulfilling, you know. I mean, I thought that I would be doing something important. Women go out in their business suits and have their power lunches and I know that it's not real, that it's just television, but I thought it would be something like that, you know?"

I try to ignore the fact that I am here talking about how shitty my life is to someone who just spent years behind bars and just keep going. But if anyone were to understand this, it would be him.

"What is it like?" Owen asks.

"It's...boring," I say with a shrug. "I don't know how else to put it. It's dreary. I go into the office every morning, go through my emails, and then stare at my phone for about an hour before forcing myself to get to work. Work involves making up math questions for these standardized tests they are making kids take in school. The fucked up thing is that the point of them is to not even evaluate the kids but to see whether the teachers are teaching to the tests well enough to keep their jobs."

Owen waves over to the waitress to refill his coffee cup.

"Nothing about it has anything to do with real learning. They could teach kids how to do these problems the easy way but they want to sell textbooks and testing materials to schools so they came up with all of this new type of math that's confusing even for me to write, let alone for kids to learn. The teachers are forced to just teach to these tests to keep their jobs and my job is to just perpetuate this whole cycle."

"So...what I'm getting from you is that you're unfulfilled by your work," Owen says and we both burst out laughing.

"I shouldn't complain about it. It's dumb," I say. "You're the one with the real problems."

"No, that's not true," Owen says. "There are no dumb problems. This is your experience and this is something important that you're going through."

I smile at him and reach across the table to put my hand over his.

"How did you get so smart?" I ask, giving it a little squeeze.

"It's amazing what a little reading can do for you," he says.

## 5

## NICHOLAS
### WHEN I WATCH HER...

After Art leaves, I get into my car and sit here for a while staring at the light flickering above my head.

What do I do now? If I want to keep Art happy, I have to do what he says.

But that means betraying Olive because Owen is her brother and they are very close.

I don't know the parameters of the job that Art has for me but making friends with Owen isn't a good sign. The details aren't important right now because I already know the storyline.

Art needs me to get close to Owen so

that Owen starts to trust me. Art needs Owen to trust me so that I can be placed in the position to betray him. This is the story of my life ever since I'd lost Lance.

Growing up you are either the kid who thinks about his future or you're not.

Television would make you believe that most of us are those who do think about it, but my experience tells me that most of us don't. Otherwise no one would be drug dealers or gang bangers or prostitutes. These professions are just one of those things that happen to people as they make choices in life that make sense at the moment.

Planning one's life is for the privileged.

Or maybe not. Maybe that's just some bullshit story I tell myself to make my life make sense, to not feel like such a stranger all the time.

The truth is that I rarely gave my own future any thought.

My mother was never the type to ask "Honey, what do you want to do when you grow up?" Hell, she was never the type to call me honey.

She was too busy popping pills and shouting at one of her boyfriends to care.

The only thing I ever thought about as a kid was how nice it would be to be rich. I had a neighbor once, a girl a year younger, and she was just as poor as I was.

Her lights often got turned off because her parents couldn't make the bills yet that never seemed to bother her.

Armed with a library card, she had free access to all the books that she could read and that was enough for her.

She seemed to exist on another plane from the rest of us.

Kids made fun of her for not having the right clothes and for the holes her toes had worn through in her sneakers and yet when I asked her about it, she just shrugged it off.

If it were anyone else, I'd say they were lying.

But this girl wasn't.

She had her stories and that was more than enough.

I wish I could have been like her. I wish that I didn't crave power and wealth and a short cut to both.

To be rich meant having people look up to you and not worrying about the heat being turned off.

In my neighborhood, the only people who had anything like that were drug dealers and gang bangers.

Since I didn't want to be either, I developed a set of special skills. With my partner and best friend, Lance Bredinsky, I perfected them.

The last job that Lance and I did was take a two-million dollar Harry Winston necklace off a couple from Martha's Vineyard. This necklace was going to set us up for life.

Our boss had no idea we were doing any jobs on our own, let alone anything that big. At least, that's what we thought.

Our plan was to sell the necklace, lay low for a few years, live within our means, and begin life under new identities somewhere out west.

And for a bit there, everything went according to plan.

The couple came back home and didn't notice a thing.

We had replaced the necklace with an exact replica made by a crystal artisan out of Roanoke and the wife was even photographed wearing that gaudy thing to some ball in the Hamptons.

It was a win-win. We got rich and the mark never even noticed that anything was taken.

But then a dog walker found Lance's body in the marsh. The people who bought the necklace had just wired 1.2 million dollars to our Swiss bank account which was set up in both of our new names and we had just celebrated our feat at a low-key dinner at Denny's.

Who killed him and why I still don't know until this day.

What I do know is that I'm everyone's number one suspect.

I start the car and drive over to Olive's

apartment building. I find a parking spot right outside and watch her walk around her living room. I don't see Owen but I know he's there.

How am I supposed to make this work?

How am I supposed to get him to trust me again? How am I supposed to deceive the woman who I might be falling in love with?

But what choice do I have?

The FBI has a long file on my misdeeds and if I don't cooperate I will be put away for a very long time.

No, I have to play along.

For now, anyway. First, I need to figure out what to do.

It takes a long time to come up with a good plan.

It takes research and determination.

It takes a commitment.

For now, I will become his friend. If I want to be there to protect Olive, I need to make Owen trust me.

Whoever he turned in is still after him and I have to be near Olive to help

her in case anything like what happened
before happens again.

I WILL PUT myself in their inner circle so
that I can
     be there.
     I take a deep breath and step outside.

## 6

## OLIVE

### WHEN THERE'S A KNOCK ON THE DOOR...

Back at my apartment, Owen and I indulge in a few drinks. Now that he's out on parole, he is on probation, which comes with its own set of rules.

Find meaningful employment.

No hanging out with criminals.

No leaving the city.

No drugs and no alcohol.

Owen is supposed to check in with his parole officer tomorrow morning, so these rules aren't set in stone yet.

A beer or two won't hurt anything, right?

"I can't believe that I now get a buzz after only three beers," Owen says. "You should've seen how many it took back in the day."

"I'm not sure if that's something you should be proud of," I say, laughing, finishing my second.

"I'm not drinking anymore after this," he says, cracking open the top of another bottle. "I'm not going to be one of those idiots who goes back in there because he doesn't know how to follow the rules of parole. I'm going to follow all of them to the T, you know what I mean?"

I nod and smile.

"And I'll be here for you," I say.

"But ten years is a long time to go without a drop of booze," he adds, taking another sip. I agree but I also know that he can't have anymore tonight.

"Okay, this is it," I insist. "You don't want to show up to your probation officer tomorrow morning with a hangover."

"Parole officer and probation officer aren't the same thing," he says, laughing and nodding his head in agreement.

It takes me a second to process this statement.

"Wait, what?" I ask through my alcohol-induced haze.

I'm not much of a drinker, even consuming one drink a little too fast makes me a bit weak at the knees.

"Don't look so horrified," Owen jokes. "Most people don't know. Why would they? Probation and parole officers have similar duties but parole officers deal with people who have been released from prison and probation officers supervise those who have been sentenced to serve probation instead of being incarcerated."

I stare at him for second letting all of that sink in.

"Okay, I get that, but let me ask you something else," I say.

"Shoot."

"Why do you all start to speak in this formal police talk?"

He furrows his brows in confusion.

"Like instead of car, you say it's a vehicle. Instead of woman, it's a female. You know, formal words like that?"

Owen twists his lips to one side

demonstratively thinking about the answer.

"I guess it's 'cause we spend way too much time with cops," he says and we both chuckle.

Owen and I laugh for a very long time this evening.

Whatever worries I had going into this day have all disappeared.

He's exactly the person who I grew to love over the course of our emails, only he's even better than I had imagined him to be.

He's fun.

He has a good sense of humor.

He knows exactly what to say to lighten the mood.

He doesn't take himself too seriously.

"So, you must be itching to go out and have some fun," I say after a moment. "Like girl fun, I mean."

"You mean with a girl who isn't my sister?" he jokes.

I shrug. "I know that I'm a total blast to hang out with but I know you have...needs."

"Oh my God, you make me sound like a total douche."

"I'm not saying that women don't have needs. Christ, if I had spent that much time in prison, the one thing that I would really want to do is get laid."

Owen shakes his head.

"What? Am I wrong?" I ask.

"No, you're not *wrong*. I just ...can't believe that I'm talking about this with my *sister*."

"Eh, what are siblings for, right?"

We laugh.

"Okay, I'm going to tell you something now," Owen says, taking another sip of his beer. "But you have to promise that you'll never tell anyone about this. Ever."

"Yeah, sure," I mumble.

"Olive, I'm serious. You really need to promise."

I take a moment to gather my composure. Forcing the inquisitive smile off my face, I give him a stern nod.

"Okay, yes, I won't tell a soul."

"Yes, I do want to get laid, but...I wasn't exactly celibate inside."

"Oh, really!" My eyebrows pop up to the middle of my forehead. "Who was it? Your cellmate? A guy down the hall?"

"Okay, don't get too excited!" Owen laughs.

"Dammit." I smile. "So...what's with all the intrigue?"

"I sort of had this thing with...my teacher."

My mouth drops open.

"She started working there about a year ago and we started flirting with each other and then one thing led to another."

"Oh my God," I whisper. "Are you serious?"

He nods.

"So, have you two...done *it*?"

Owen laughs, nodding.

"Seriously? But how? I thought there were cameras everywhere."

"You'd be surprised at how secretive inmates can get after a few years on the inside. And no, there aren't cameras everywhere and not all cameras are being watched all the time. That's how people get killed and...laid."

"So, what is she like?" I ask.

He thinks about it for a moment, looking for just the right word. "Sweet. Innocent. But not on the outside."

Not sure of what that means exactly, I cock my head to one side.

"She has this hard shell," Owen explains. "Stronger and more difficult to get through than most of the men I met in there. She doesn't take any shit and she doesn't play games."

"So, how did she end up falling for you?"

"Very funny." He rolls his eyes and smiles. But the expression on his face gets serious. "We were just talking one day about the Count of Monte Cristo. I was really proud of myself for reading the whole book. It is well over a thousand pages. I was really inspired by the story about this poor illiterate man who got convicted of a crime he didn't commit, sent to an awful prison where he was subjected to the worst cruelty a man could suffer...and how despite all of that he learned to read and to *learn* and started a whole new life for himself."

"There was a bit about him finding some treasure and getting revenge on everyone who had ever wronged him," I add with a smile.

"Yeah, those parts didn't hurt either." He grins. "Anyway, we were talking about that and I touched her hand and then I leaned over and kissed her."

"You did?" My eyes light up as I lean toward him to hear more details.

"Yeah, I did. It just sort of happened. I had no idea I even had feelings for her until that point and then I couldn't stop thinking about her."

"So, what about now?" I ask.

"I don't know," he says with a shrug. "We'll see."

I wrap my arms around my brother and hug him as tightly as I can. He has been through so much pain and suffering and now things are finally turning around for him.

"Everything will be fine from now on," I whisper. "I just know it."

A loud knock on the door pushes me away from him.

My heart sinks into the bottom of my stomach.

Who could that be?

## 7

## OLIVE
### WHEN THINGS ESCALATE...

W alking over to the front door, I hold my breath. If it's someone coming to do us harm then they wouldn't knock, right?

They would just burst in.

I stand up on my tiptoes to look out of the peephole. A sigh of relief washes over me just as another wave of anxiety sweeps up.

It's not a stranger coming to kill him (or me), but it's not anyone I want to see now either.

"Olive, I have to talk to you," Nicholas says.

"I can't right now. Go away," I say and walk away.

He knocks again.

And again.

"It's him, isn't it?" Owen asks.

"Just ignore him."

"Why is he *here*?"

"I don't know." I shrug.

"Is he stalking you?" Owen asks.

I furrow my brows and look at him in disbelief.

"No." I shake my head.

"So, why is he here?"

"Because he's my fucking boyfriend and we had a fight."

When I turn away from him, I roll my eyes. Nicholas' continuous knock thunders into the apartment.

"Go away! I'll call you tomorrow!" I yell.

"I need to talk to you!" he yells.

"No, you don't. I have company."

I pick up the plates and the beer bottles from the coffee table and before I can place them into the sink, Owen opens the door.

The world starts to move in slow motion.

Before I can let go of the dishes, my body turns toward the foyer in an effort to stop the inevitable.

Nicholas isn't supposed to be here because he knows that Owen is staying with me.

That's why I didn't let him in.

I wanted to keep them apart until I could figure out a more delicate way to deal with all of this. But now…

The plates hit the floor with a bang, making both Owen and Nicholas jump.

But the sound doesn't faze me.

I step over the mess and walk closer to them.

"I don't want to talk right now," I say, my voice cracking in the middle of the plea. "I'll call you tomorrow."

"Listen, I just wanted to come by and apologize," Nicholas says quickly. "I'm so sorry. I should have never put you in that position. I was a selfish asshole."

"What else is new?" Owen says under his breath.

My eyes widen expecting a blow back from Nicholas.

But much to my surprise he doesn't take the bait.

"Hi, I'm Nicholas," he says, extending his hand. "You must be Owen."

"You don't remember me, do you?" Owen asks, crossing his arms.

Nicholas leaves his hand out in the open for a moment before putting it back into his pocket.

"Of course, I do," Nicholas says, meeting his eyes.

They glare at each other so hard that I wait for bolts of electricity to surge in between them. "I just thought that I would introduce myself to start on better footing."

"I'm not interested in starting anything again," Owen says. "My sister asked you to leave, so leave."

Nicholas takes a deep breath.

I hate the way that he asked him but I want Nicholas to do as he was told.

This isn't the right time for this.

But instead, he waltzes past both of us and kneels over the broken dishes.

"I'll get that, it's fine," I start to say when he is already carrying them to the garbage can.

"I'm sorry I startled you," he whispers.

"You have to leave," I whisper back.

Owen and I have talked about almost everything and anything today except what is really important.

I wonder now if that was a mistake.

He has only a few glimpses of my relationship with Nicholas and I know nothing about why he was really released.

Did he really turn on someone?

Is that person out for blood? Or did Nicholas just fill my head with lies?

"Well, I guess I'll talk to you tomorrow then," Nicholas says and a wave of relief washes over me.

"Yes, sure, of course." I stumble over my words.

"Or maybe I can just stay for a drink?" he asks in his flirtatious way. He isn't imposing. He's just putting out an idea. No pressure, right?

"That is not a good idea. It's getting late, and Olive has work in the morning," Owen steps in. I don't know if he's trying to be helpful or just trying to assert his territory, in either case he is in over his head.

"No, she doesn't," Nicholas says, nonchalantly. I turn around and give him a stern look, but it's not enough to make him stop talking.

Turning to him, he explains, "We don't have work tomorrow. So, you two can spend the day together if you want."

Owen looks at me. I don't say a word.

"What does he mean by '*we*'?"

I don't reply.

It's none of his business.

I don't have to explain myself to anyone. I'm not a child.

"I thought you worked writing test questions for an educational company?" Owen asks.

"That's what I used to do," I finally say

when the silence becomes too unbearable.

I go over the reasons why I no longer wanted to work there again even though I doubt that he cares.

He focuses his attention entirely on Nicholas.

While Owen scowls, Nicholas paints a plastic half-smile on his face which gives his expression a mixture of something in between acquiesce and contempt.

"So, what is it that you're doing now?" Owen asks me quietly. "Working for him?"

I nod slightly.

"Doing what exactly? Lying? Scamming? Defrauding people? Or have you two moved on to something else now?"

"What are you talking about?" I demand to know, anger rising deep within me.

"Anyone show up dead yet?" Owen asks, his voice drenched in condensation.

Shivers run up my spine. What is he talking about? What does he know? Is he referring to Caitlyn or the man who tried to take me?

"You need to calm down, Owen," I say. "I don't owe you a fucking explanation."

"Yes, you do. Especially if you're going to hang out with the likes of him."

"There's nothing wrong with him," I insist. "He didn't just spend a decade in prison."

"Fuck you, Olive. I'm just trying to look after you."

"She doesn't need you to look after her," Nicholas pipes in.

"Shut up! Both of you!" I shout over them. "I don't know who you think you are but you can't just barge into my life and start telling me what to do. I've been an adult for a long time now, making my own decisions."

I walk over to Nicholas and put my hand on his chest. "Please leave," I say quietly. "He's my brother and he has nowhere else to go."

"Don't throw me a pity party, will you?" Owen says from across the room.

"Shut up!" I hiss at him.

Nicholas gives me a nod and allows me to walk him across the room.

When we reach Owen in the foyer, it takes him a minute to move out of the way.

"Can I see you tomorrow?" Nicholas asks.

"No, you can't," Owen answers for me.

"Shut up," I say and turn back toward Nicholas. "I don't know. Maybe."

"Please? I have to talk to you about something."

"Listen, man, she already said no. Can't you take that for an answer?" Owen says, shoving his finger in the air.

"Why don't you get that out of my fucking face?" Nicholas says, grabbing it with his hand.

A second later, one of them throws a punch and a full blown fight begins.

## 8

## OLIVE
### WHEN THINGS ESCALATE...

Once they start throwing punches, I can barely sneak past them without getting hit. They make only some nominal space for me to escape and once I'm out, their fists continue the attack on each other's bodies.

"Stop it! Stop fighting!" I yell at the top of my lungs.

When I make a move to separate them, an elbow collides with my shoulder tossing me into the wall.

"Look what you did!" one of them screams.

"You are the one who made me do it!" the other yells.

The pain in my shoulder runs up and down my arm and I can't help but lean against the wall and slide down to the floor.

This seems to do the trick because they both crowd on top of me with concerned expressions on their faces.

"You're both assholes," I whisper through my teeth.

"It was all his fault," they say simultaneously. I shake my head and try to rise back up to my feet. But Owen pushes me back down.

"Get away from her," Nicholas says. "Can't you see that she's trying to stand up?"

"Don't touch me!" Owen roars back.

With no more energy to devote to them, I slide out of the way keeping my back to the wall and my butt on the floor.

Once I have enough space, I wince and force myself to my feet.

I get all the way to the kitchen before either of them notices that I am gone.

When they finally do, they race over to me.

"Stay away," I say to both of them at the same time.

My eyes dart from one confused face to another.

Owen opens his mouth to say something, but I put my index finger up to his lips.

"I'm so..." Nicholas manages to get out before I shut him down as well.

"I'm sick of you," I finally say when I have their full attention. "Both of you."

I pause and wait for them to speak up but now they both know better.

"Owen, I quit my job because I hated it. Nicholas' offer was just the impetus I needed to do something...dangerous," I say.

Nicholas smiles at Owen with a smug expression of satisfaction.

"Nicholas, you made me an offer I couldn't refuse but that doesn't mean that you get to tell me what to do. We are partners and if I don't want to do a particular job then I won't do it."

He doesn't respond.

"Owen, you can stay here for as long

as you want and nothing that Nicholas says will change that. But if you want to stay in my life," I say, pointing my finger at Nicholas, "you have to accept the fact that Owen is my brother and you can never change what we have."

Now, it's Owen's turn to smile at Nicholas with a look of self-righteousness.

I choose to ignore both of them for a moment and focus on the pain that's manifesting in my shoulder.

I open the freezer and take out a bag of frozen asparagus.

I pull down my long sleeve shirt and place the cold packet as close to the point of impact as I can reach.

Seeing me struggle, Owen and Nicholas both offer to help but I give them each a stern "no, thank you." I don't want to side with either of them in order to appear as neutral as possible.

When my shoulder not so much gets better but just goes numb, I put the bag back into the freezer and pour myself a new cup of tea.

I want to ask Nicholas to leave but I'm afraid that doing so would only make me look like I'm siding with Owen.

In reality, I am glad that he's here.

I hated the way we had left things and I wish that I could broker some sort of peace between the two most important men in my life.

As that thought crosses my mind, I pause and give it some consideration.

When I was a little kid, I was really close to my father. He was a competitive swimmer in high school and he used to take me to the YMCA pool all the time.

Being in water relaxed him like nothing else and he was the one who taught me how to swim with goggles on when I was only eighteen months.

He did so with Owen and our older brother, too, but I was the one who really loved being there as much as he did.

For months after my dad walked out of our lives, I went to the pool to mourn him.

He wasn't dead (as far as I knew) so he

didn't have a gravestone or another place I could mourn his passing.

He did have a favorite bar but they didn't let in kids so the YMCA pool was all I had.

I would take the bus and then swim laps until my arms and legs and lungs were physically exhausted.

Then I would swim some more.

After Dad left, I had no more male figures in my life. My brothers were strangers to me and I was only glad when my mom's fleeting boyfriends didn't take an interest in me.

They always moved in on their second date, they rarely had jobs, and they left as soon as our electricity or cable got cut off, which was pretty often.

Eventually, I learned how to disconnect the lights myself to get the ones who hit her to leave early.

But now things are different, aren't they? I have two men in my life who want to be here.

They want what's best for me even if

they don't agree to what that is. I would be lying if I said that it didn't feel good.

The only problem is that if they don't get along then I won't have them in my life for long.

I will have to choose between them and that's not a choice that I want to make.

The doorbell buzzes.

I stare into the foyer wondering who that could be since it's well after six.

"Ms. Kernes!" A deep voice accompanies the loud knock. "Ms. Kernes, it's the police. We have a few questions for you."

## 9

## OLIVE

### WHEN THEY ASK QUESTIONS...

Something gets lodged somewhere in the back of my throat. I try to breathe in or out but I can't do either.

My eyes open wide as I stare at the door.

Don't open it.

Just pretend that no one is home.

But they continue to knock.

"Ms. Kernes, please open the door," the cop says.

There is no urgency in the tone of his voice.

It's calm.

Direct.

Confident.

"What does he want?" I whisper to Nicholas.

He shakes his head.

"I don't know," he says under his breath and walks toward them.

"Where are you going?" I leap over to him and grab his arm. "No, we're not home," I add in a loud whisper, loud enough for the man on the other side of the door to hear.

"We know you're there, Ms. Kernes. We just have a few questions."

My hands drop to my sides and all the blood pools somewhere in between my toes.

"It's going to be fine," Nicholas says inaudibly. "Just follow my lead."

When he touches his hand to the doorknob, he pauses for a moment and looks back.

But he's not looking at me.

Instead, his gaze focuses entirely on Owen who is as white as a sheet.

"Are you ready?" Nicholas mouths to him.

Owen waits a second before giving him a nod.

"Hello, officers. How can we help you?" Nicholas asks in a sing-song almost chipper voice.

"Nicky?" one of the officers asks, leaning closer to him.

Nicholas' shoulders tense and rise an inch before he relaxes them.

The officer is in his early thirties but looks older.

He is overweight with sallow skin and big black circles around his eyes.

His hair is somehow both dry and oily and unkept.

"My God, Docky!" Nicholas says, wrapping his arms around the man's shoulders.

I glance over at Owen who looks just as confused as I do by this turn of events.

"What the hell are you doing here?" Officer Docky says. "Benji, this is Nicky. He was one of my best friends growing up."

The taller, thinner officer who is clearly no stranger to the gym introduces himself as Benjamin Inglese to not only Nicholas but also to Owen and me.

"So, how did you know each other?" I ask Nicholas, hoping that this connection is something that will make whatever reason they are here to see me go away.

"We knew each other when we were, what, eleven? We were pretty inseparable then."

"Yeah, and then this son of a bitch moved away and I never heard from him again," Officer Docky says.

"Hey, that wasn't my fault, we got evicted, remember?"

"They had phones across town, too, you know," Officer Docky says with a tinge of sorrow.

"Yeah, but we didn't," Nicholas says, patting him on the back. "Seriously, I'm so sorry that we lost touch. I had your number for a while and then I lost it and, it's not like there was a Facebook or anything back then. And I was just a stupid kid."

"Yeah, I get it...it's so good to see you again, man!"

Officer Docky is smiling from ear to ear.

Nicholas is, too, but he's not pretending or playing along as I had thought.

He is smiling with his whole face.

Even his eyes shine.

"Hi, I'm Olive Kernes," I say, extending my hand.

Nicholas makes the introduction. Officer Docky's real name is Carillion Dockery.

"Please call me Dockery, everyone does," he adds, shaking Owen's hand after mine.

"Not Docky?" I joke.

He shakes his head from side to side.

"No one has called me that since I was in middle school."

"I'm not so sure how true that is," Nicholas says with a smile at the corner of his lips.

"Would you two want to come in and have something to drink?" I offer.

Nicholas flashes a disapproving glare in my direction, but I ignore it.

The history that has flooded into the hallway makes it impossible for me to not invite the two officers inside.

I have nothing to hide so I have to act like it.

Besides, I don't even know what they are here to ask me.

"We're technically on the job," Dockery says, "otherwise I'd love to have a drink and catch up."

"Tea or coffee then?" I offer.

Officer Inglese and Owen agree to coffee and I start to make a fresh pot.

When I hand out the cups, the casual chitchat starts to die down.

Dockery finishes his story about how skinny and uncoordinated Nicholas was as a kid and doesn't start another one.

Instead, he and Inglese exchange glances and give each other a knowing nod.

"Okay, so the reason we're here," Dockery starts, "is that we had some questions for you, Olive."

I take a sip of my tea.

"Do you know a man by the name of Louis Prang?"

I shake my head no.

"Are you sure?" Inglese asks.

I think about it again, but the name doesn't ring a bell.

"Where were you on Thursday, the 19th?" Dockery asks.

"What is with all of the questions?" Nicholas asks, buying me some time to think about the answer.

"I don't know. I was home I guess, but I'm not sure."

Dockery and Inglese exchange looks.

"Can you tell us what's going on?" Owen asks.

"Louis Prang was seen going into your building and one of your neighbors saw him knocking on your door," Inglese says.

He is leaning over in his seat and peering into my eyes, trying to get a read on my reaction.

I have an urge to make fists out of my hands but I know that I have to remain as calm and unfazed as possible.

"I don't know why," I say, shrugging my shoulders. "I have no idea who he is."

"So, you had no one come to your door that evening? No one at all?"

I run my tongue over the roof of my mouth.

"Um...actually, yes," I say.

Nicholas places his hand on the small of my back in an effort to shut me up, but I know what I'm doing. "A woman came by to buy a rug. I don't remember her name but I think I have her card here somewhere."

Nicholas' hand relaxes and gives me a pat.

"A woman bought a rug from you?" Dockery asks, looking over at Inglese. I nod.

"Yeah, so what? Why? Who is Louis Prang? Did something happen to him?"

"Yes, his body was recently found in Boston Harbor," Inglese says and my head starts to pound.

I f the police officers are examining my face for a look of surprise, they are going to see it.

I try to hide it as much as possible but I'm not sure that it's effective.

Suddenly, a spark of an idea hits me.

"I'm sorry I'm just a little startled by this whole thing," I say, rubbing the back of my neck. If I can't hide my state of shock I can just lean into it.

"This has been quite an emotional day with my brother getting out of prison...so, I guess what I'm saying is that...what does this have to do with me?"

"Well, your neighbor did see someone knock on your door," Dockery says.

"I really have no idea who he is or why he was here," I say, shrugging so demonstratively that I feel like my shoulders are going to touch my ears.

"If he was even here," Nicholas says.

Dockery narrows his eyes.

"Well, you know, eyewitness reports are wrong all the time. He might have been the delivery guy or someone from the moving company."

Nicholas goes on to explain that the woman who bought the rug brought along two moving guys to help her transport it.

He gives them an accurate description of them along with the woman's card, which he fishes out of his pocket but makes it look like it fell out from under the magazines laying on the coffee table.

This seems to satisfy them and they leave on a high note.

"So, what was that about?" Owen asks, glaring at Nicholas. "You did something to get her in trouble, didn't you?"

Owen doesn't know the details of any of this, but Nicholas doesn't need to tell me to keep my mouth shut.

He killed a man who tried to attack me but we never called the police and reported it.

The less Owen knows about any of this the better.

Nicholas lets out a deep breath in exasperation and walks toward the door.

"Where are you going?" I ask.

"You need to get some rest, we'll talk tomorrow."

I bite my lower lip, wanting more than anything to ask him to stay. But the timing is all wrong.

Owen is here and they don't get along.

The best thing that can happen now is to just let him go for the moment.

"I'll be right back," I tell Owen and follow Nicholas out into the hallway.

The walls are thick but I don't trust that they are thick enough to keep us safe from prying ears.

It's best not to even take the chance.

"You don't have to leave," I say, taking his arm. "I know that we both said some things that we regret last night."

"I don't regret anything."

"You don't mean that."

"Yes, I do."

"You really meant to call me a spoiled brat?"

He clenches his jaw.

"I didn't think so."

When I turn around to walk back to my door, he leaps in front of me.

I want to let him off easy but I don't dare.

If he wants my forgiveness he has to give me an actual apology.

I am not going to be one of those women who just accepts that the man's ego is too big to ever say that he's wrong.

"What do you want from me?" Nicholas asks after a moment.

My eyes meet his and I stare at the specks of gold that form around the edges of his irises.

"I want you to apologize," I say.

He looks away for a moment and then takes a deep breath.

"I'm sorry. I was wrong. I shouldn't have said that."

I give him a knowing nod.

"I'm sorry, too. I shouldn't have gotten so upset and I shouldn't have called you an asshole."

"Thank you," he whispers, taking another step closer to me.

I inhale the scent of his skin and my fingers tingle as I fight the urge to touch him.

He doesn't fight his.

Instead, he puts his hand on the back of my neck and pulls me closer to him.

Our lips touch.

Our mouths open.

Our tongues intertwine.

He buries his fingers in my hair and I run mine up the back of his spine.

Nothing else matters at this moment but us. Nothing else exists but us.

"Olive!" someone yells my name in the distance.

When he says it again, he is suddenly much closer and louder.

Reluctantly, I pull away from Nicholas and look at Owen.

Standing in the doorway with his hands crossed, he taps his foot on the floor waiting for me to come inside.

He interrupted us on purpose and he does not want to take no for an answer. "I'll call you tomorrow," I tell Nicholas, admitting defeat.

He gives me another long passionate kiss before saying, "It was a pleasure to meet you Owen!" And disappears down the hallway.

"What was that all about?" I hiss at Owen and push him back inside.

"You need to stay away from that guy," he says. "You have *no* idea who he is."

## OLIVE
WHEN WE FIGHT...

Back inside, Owen and I have the conversation that I have been dreading to have ever since I learned about his parole.

We had spent a fun day together laughing and catching up, all the while ignoring the one topic of conversation that we both knew was off limits.

When Nicholas showed up, that changed. The elephant in the room became visible and he started breaking shit.

It's late.

The cops just came and rattled me to

my core and the alcohol is still coursing its way through my system making my eyelids heavy.

But watching Owen pace back and forth in the kitchen, I know that I won't be able to put this off until tomorrow.

I walk over to the sink and turn on the water.

Waiting for it to warm up, I stare at the stream and the way it bounces off my fingertips.

"Olive, you can't be with that guy," Owen insists. "He's dangerous."

I wash a plate with the sponge and place it upside down on a towel by the sink.

I have a dishwasher right underneath but I never had one growing up and I find washing dishes to be relaxing.

"Olive, you realize what's going on here, right?" he says. "Those cops were here asking about some guy coming into your place. That means that in all likelihood, Nicholas probably killed him."

I turn toward him, glaring.

"Don't give me that look, you know I'm right."

Nicholas didn't *probably* kill him.

He killed him for a certainty, trying to protect me.

I want to tell Owen this, but I can't.

Now, it's my turn to protect Nicholas.

"You know that he made up that whole story about the rug, Olive? Right? They're going to check up on it and they're going to find out the truth."

I look up at Owen, shaking my head.

Where does he get all of this confidence?

Was he always this cocky and self-assured even if he knows absolutely nothing about my life?

"Olive, say something," he demands. "Say something so I know that you're listening."

I take a step closer.

We are only a few inches apart and I can smell the stale alcohol on his breath.

"Who do you think you are?" I say after a moment of staring into his eyes.

"What makes you think that you can speak to me as if I need your advice?"

"You're my little sister," he says.

I don't remember him ever calling me his 'little' sister and in this context, he is wielding it like a weapon.

"Don't patronize me," I say. "And Nicholas did not make up the story about the rug. I did sell it to a woman I found through her magazine ad. It was big and unwieldy so she brought a few moving people to help her carry it."

This shuts him up but only for a moment.

"It doesn't change the fact that Nicholas is a dangerous man."

I roll my eyes and walk away from him.

At the bottom of my dresser, I find clean sheets and start to make the couch into his bed for the night.

When Nicholas first told the cops the rug story, I thought that he was betraying her.

But now I realize that she's our plan B, my alibi.

She wasn't hiding the fact that she was there.

In reality, she made quite a show of it.

The neighbors saw her, too.

And she even brought the magazine with her ad inside and circled it as I would have done if any of that were true.

I pull on the pillowcase and wish him good night.

"Why would I lie about this?" Owen asks. "I'm your brother and I love you."

"I don't think you're lying. I think you're just mistaken."

"His partner ended up dead. They were best friends and he just killed him so that he could keep the whole necklace to himself."

Shivers run down my spine.

I don't know anything about this and it's possible that this part is true.

"He wouldn't do that," I say categorically, not wanting Owen to know that I have even a glimmer of doubt.

"Yes, he would," Owen insists. "He did lots of bad things, Olive, I know that you don't want to believe that but he did."

The conversation is going in circles, sapping me from energy with each passing minute.

Owen doesn't stop talking until I close my bedroom door in his face.

I hate to admit it but Owen is right.

I don't really know much about Nicholas' past, but a part of me doesn't really want to.

What if he did kill his partner?

Is that something that I even want to know?

These thoughts swirl around my head deep into the night.

Eventually, I do fall asleep but it is not particularly restful or fulfilling.

I wake up even more tired than I was before, only this time I am also parched.

After gulping down two glasses of water in the bathroom, I pick up my phone. No texts from Nicholas. Damn.

*Are you up?* I write.

*No,* he texts back almost immediately. I smile.

*I want you.*

*I'll be right over.*

My fingers start to text no, but I stop myself.

*Okay.*

I run my tongue over my lower lip.

A part of me thinks that he is joking, but I still change out of my pajamas.

Fifteen minutes later, my phone vibrates again.

*I'm downstairs.*

I open the door to my bedroom carefully and tiptoe through the living room.

I grasp onto the keys in my hand so hard that my palm starts to throb and I wonder if there's going to be a mark.

The problem is the front door. It squeaks.

I inhale and turn the bolt lock to the right.

If Owen were to wake up, he would be in the perfect position to witness my escape.

But he lets out a big snore and turns toward the inside of the couch.

Without wasting another second, I open the door and shut it quickly behind me.

"Hey, stranger," I say, getting into Nicholas' car. "I've missed you."

# 12

## OLIVE

Dressed in a black tie and dress shirt, his eyes are a perfect complement to his tie. My heart rate speeds up and my lips part in surprise.

There's an alluring smell to him.

It's not cologne or body wash, it is something else completely different.

He smells like the Nicholas Crawford I met in Hawaii: shrewd, assertive, and confident.

My mouth waters for him.

When he reaches over to give me a kiss, I catch a glimpse of his white gold cufflinks and the diamond studded watch.

Our lips touch and I hear the pounding of my pulse in my head.

The electricity sends shockwaves through me.

He's no stranger and yet I feel like I'm seeing him for the first time.

"Are you okay?" he asks, pulling away from the curb.

He puts his hand on my thigh and every part of me yearns for him. I'm filled with restless energy that only one thing can fix.

"Yes, I'm fine," I say, licking my dry lips. "Why are you dressed like this?"

Despite the fight with Owen and the conversation with the cops only a few hours ago, Nicholas looks like a Master of the Universe type.

Perfectly pressed pants.

Exquisite suit.

Tie with a tie clip.

His hair is slicked back with product, but not so much to make him appear desperate.

"What's going on with us?" I ask.

This isn't the best time for this conversation but I was under the impression that we were going to go to a hotel.

And now, I'm not so sure.

"What do you mean?" he asks, stepping on the accelerator to rush through the intersection when the light turns yellow.

"I hate to say it but I thought this was going to be something of a booty call."

"Oh, you did?" he says, raising one eyebrow. I shrug. "And now?"

"Well, now I see you dressed like this and I'm not so sure."

He smiles out of the corner of his lips.

He is toying with me and he likes it.

We haven't played this game for a while and I have missed it.

Does he want me?

Do I want him?

These questions don't matter.

What matters is what am I going to do to him.

And what is he going to do to me?

I want to press the matter further but instead I sit back in my seat and wait. I am okay with any eventuality.

Another job? I am dressed in yoga pants and a sweatshirt with a tea stain down one arm, but why the hell not? I'm down.

Nicholas turns up the music as we drive down the winding empty streets.

The cobblestones underneath the tires make the ride bumpy, arousing me even more, if that were possible.

"Pull over," I say, running my hand up his thigh.

He smiles again without saying a word.

"We're almost there," he says after a moment.

I move my hand but he puts it back in place.

He wants me as much as I want him.

Is that even possible?

We pull into an opulent old hotel with an elaborate awning.

An eager valet runs around the front

of the car to get the door for Nicholas and another opens mine.

After the keys are exchanged, I follow Nicholas through the elegant double doors that another person opens for us.

We are a study in opposites.

Nicholas is dressed in an understated but very expensive suit along with stacked heel, seamed toe, leather shoes.

When he moves his arms, his cufflinks catch the light and blind me for a moment.

When I move my arms, my oversized sweatshirt with the cut off collar makes a loud chaffing sound.

I'm wearing thirty-dollar tennis shoes that I got on sale and debated whether I had paid too much for.

My stringy and unwashed hair is tied up in a loose bun with a fifty-cent scrunchy.

I was relieved when they came back into fashion because they don't pull my hair as much as regular hair ties and I think they look nice knotted around my wrist.

I follow Nicholas toward the elevators and take his hand into mine while we wait.

"Is this a job?" I ask.

"What do you think?" he asks, wrapping his hands around my hand.

"If it were, I would've thought you would at least have the courtesy to tell me something about it," I point out. He smiles.

"Let's put it this way, it's a job for you."

My lips form into a smile.

What could he mean by that?

He gazes into my eyes.

I stare back trying to read them.

"I told you, I'm not going to be with you as part of any..." I pause, trying to find the right word.

"Yes?" he prompts me.

"I'm not going to bed with you as part of any *offer*."

"You mean, I get to sleep with you for...free?" He mocks me. I roll my eyes in desperation. Why does he have to be so...smart? I guess, if he weren't then I wouldn't want him so much.

He's attractive, of course.

But that is not enough for me.

If he didn't say things that took me aback and surprised me then I wouldn't be here.

I wouldn't crave him so much.

He grabs me as soon as we reach the door.

He presses me against the wall and I wrap my legs around him.

He tries to stick the card into the reader while we kiss without much success.

Finally, I push him away for a moment, grab the card, and slide it down.

When the green light comes on, I open the door.

We practically run over to the bed.

It's tall and I bounce as I toss myself onto it. Nicholas jumps on top of me and our bodies collide.

The impact makes us both laugh.

"It's nice to be here with you," Nicholas says, after a moment.

The laughter disappears, leaving only

the remnants of a smile on his lips and in his eyes.

"I like it here," I say.

He turns his body on his side, propping his head up with his hand. He uses the other to move a strand of hair off my cheek.

"So...what are we, Olive?" he asks, examining the strand carefully as if he is looking for split ends.

"What do you mean?" I ask, pulling my hair away from him and sitting up with my legs crossed.

"I like you, Olive. A lot."

"Well...thank you," I say, keenly aware of how different the mood suddenly is.

"Do you like me?"

"Yes."

"Do you like other people?"

I look up at the unmoving blades of the ceiling fan above our heads.

"I don't know what you are getting at," I say.

"I'm just wondering where this is going," Nicholas says, sitting up next to me.

"I don't know. I thought I was working with you. I thought we were partners."

"We are," he agrees. "I was just wondering if you wanted to be anything more than that?"

## 13

## OLIVE
### WHEN WE KISS AGAIN ...

Is he really asking me this? I wonder.

"Do you want to be exclusive?" I ask.

"Yes," he says without a second of hesitation.

I want to smile but I keep it to myself. I want to hear more.

"Why?" I ask.

"I want you. I don't want anyone else to have you."

"So...what would that mean then?"

"It means I want you to be mine. Officially."

I lie down on my back, thinking about the proposition.

What is he asking me really?

"So, do you want me to be your girlfriend?" I ask. "Is this what you're saying?"

He leans over to me and turns my chin toward his.

"I want you to be mine," he says.

A cold shiver runs down my spine as the hairs on the back of my arm stand upright.

"What about the offer?" I ask.

"Professionally, you would still be my partner for a year, but in our personal life, we would be more than that."

I want him to say the word girlfriend but he is just dancing around the topic. But maybe that's not what he means at all. Maybe he wants me to be his without him being mine?

"What about you?" I ask.

His eyes meet mine. He tilts his head.

"What if I don't want anyone else to have you either?" I ask.

"No one else will. I'm yours."

"So...that's it?" I ask. "Neither of us will date anyone else from this point on?"

He nods and brings his face closer to mine.

"I am yours and you are mine," he whispers.

My lips part to welcome his. Our tongues touch. He buries his hand in my hair and pulls me down underneath him.

I put my thoughts aside and let my body take over.

One moment, his lips are on my mouth and the next they are moving down my neck.

One moment, his hands are in my hair and the next they are moving down my back.

My eyes close as I press my body against his. Heat radiates from his skin, engulfing mine, only flaming my desire for him.

When his lips come back to mine, our kisses quicken with need as our mouths work hard to consume one another's.

My hands run down his body.

His chest moves up and down with each breath and the muscles in his tight stomach flex and relax.

Whatever thoughts occupied my mind only moments before disappear as I lose myself in anticipation of what's about to come.

My hand slides down the front of his pants and as I unzip the front, I know that he's as aroused as I am.

We have been here so many times before.

All of the almost-moments and all of the interruptions have taken a toll and now I don't want to waste a second.

The way that Nicholas is taking off my clothes, I know that I am not alone. The way he snaps on the condom, I know that we both want the same thing.

I lick my parched lips as his lips run down my body. His are both soft and firm and there's a gentleness with which he kisses first my collarbone, then my breasts, my stomach, and finally right along my panty line.

I bury my hands in his hair as his kisses become more fervent and urgent. I want him to linger and to take his time but another part of me doesn't want to tempt fate.

Of all the times we have been together, almost together, we have never gone all the way. I can't handle another temptation.

I will not stand for another tease.

I tug at his hair and pull his chin upward so that our eyes meet again.

"Come here," I whisper and pull his face back up to mine.

I direct his mouth to mine and lose myself in a deepening kiss.

With his chest on top of mine, I listen to our raging heartbeats, not sure which one belongs to him and which one to me.

I open my legs for him and he pushes himself deep inside. My back arches as we start to move as one.

My skin is damp and hot, filled with electricity.

My breasts bounce as we rock back and forth. My legs spread further apart with each breath and my toes tense up. The steady pace suddenly speeds up.

My heart starts to beat faster and

faster along with each thrust. A familiar tingling starts at the tips of my hands and rushes quickly throughout my body.

I grab onto his smooth, strong buttocks and push him deeper inside of me. The warm sensation catches me by surprise as my body clenches up to hold on for the ride.

A moment later, he collapses on top of me, also completely spent.

## 14

### OLIVE

WHEN WE FIGHT...

I stay the night in Nicholas' hotel room and only go home in the morning. I wake up around seven to get back to the apartment before Owen wakes up.

But as soon as I step through the front door, I see him.

He's wide awake, sitting at the dining room table, waiting.

The television isn't on and there isn't a book in sight.

"Where were you?" he asks in the tone of a concerned father.

Not mine but the ones I've only seen on the screen.

I drop my bag on the floor and head straight to the coffee pot without saying a word.

"Didn't you hear me?" he asks.

"I don't owe you an explanation, Owen. I'm a grown woman."

"I was worried."

I shrug my shoulders. "You have no right to be worried."

A part of me is flattered by his protectiveness.

It shows that he cares.

At least, that's what we women have been trained to believe. But another part sees it as controlling.

The only reason he is claiming that he's worried is because he has a bad history with Nicholas.

"I don't understand how this concerns you," I say, taking a sip of the coffee. It's way too hot, burning the roof of my mouth. But I hide the pain.

"I already told you, Olive. He's a very dangerous man. You shouldn't be working with him. And you shouldn't be sleeping with him."

"What about dating?" I ask, tilting my chin in the air. "Is dating okay?"

Owen looks as if he had the wind knocked out of him.

"Tell me that's not true," he says when he regains his ability to speak. I fold my hands across my chest.

"Yes, it is and it's none of your business," I say.

I grab my favorite seat in the wingback chair next to the living room.

This is where I like to curl up to read, but this morning, I use it like a throne.

I sit with my legs wide open, grabbing on to the arm rests with both hands.

My back is perfectly straight.

There's nothing dainty about this. It makes me feel powerful and strong.

How dare he come into my life, my home, and question my decisions?

How dare he tell me what to do?

"I just don't get it, Olive," Owen says. "I mean, what the hell do you even see in him?"

"I would answer that question if I knew that you were genuinely interested.

But you don't care. You hate him and you want me to hate him, too. Well, that's not going to happen."

"He killed his partner. Everyone knows it. Do you want to be with someone like that?"

"I don't know what happened between him and his partner, and I won't believe anything until you show me some actual proof," I say sternly.

He shakes his head.

"Fine," Owen says with exasperation, walking toward the front door. "If you want to ruin your life, fine."

"Who do you think you are? What gives you the right to tell me what to do?"

"I'm your fucking brother. I care about you. I don't want you to make a mistake."

"I haven't seen you in years," I say. "You don't know anything about me. And you come into my house and start telling me what to do? Keep your opinions to yourself, Owen."

This finally shuts him up.

He finishes his coffee and washes the cup.

He grabs the set of spare keys I gave him last night and walks out of the door.

Once he is gone, I jump up to my feet and ball up my fists.

The caffeine that is making its way through my veins amplifies my anger. I'm so angry I want to punch something.

Why does he have to be so difficult? Why can't he just get along with him?

When Nicholas showed up, he was making an effort. He was trying to be nice.

But Owen is just being so...unreasonable.

I let out a visceral, bellowing scream of frustration that originates somewhere in the pit of my stomach.

Once, I get that out of my system, I grab my iPad and flip on the last show that I was watching on Netflix. I can no longer tolerate the commercials on regular television, and streaming channels fill the void.

I subscribe to Netflix, YouTube TV,

and Amazon Prime giving me an array of old and new shows as well as movies to feed my appetite.

I start a comedy but I don't laugh. I start a drama, but their problems seem inane.

My thoughts continue to swirl around in my head and the pictures and the voices on the show are not enough to quiet them.

In the kitchen, I pour myself a cup of caffeine-free mint tea and leave the bag inside.

I go back to my favorite spot and open the Kindle app. When all else fails, this always does the trick. Books.

I love to read and I devour a few books a week. Reading seems to activate a whole other part of my brain.

With the right writer, the words just leap off the page and I have to keep turning them until I'm done.

I always liked to read growing up but I never read *this* much.

I never knew that there was this whole other world of indie books and indie writers until I discovered the Kindle.

Suddenly, I was able to read the kind of books that I have always looked for.

In traditionally published books, the sex is always cursory or non-existent. The intimate parts of the story, the ones that you really want to read about suddenly fade to black.

The few authors who do depict it, often do so using crude or clumsy language and end their novels on low notes. At least, that is my impression of contemporary literary fiction.

But with independent authors who mainly sell eBooks, the stories are completely different.

They don't shy away from private details, in fact, they lean into them. They discuss what was never discussed before and the traditional publishing success of *Fifty Shades of Grey,* the series that E. L. James first published independently, are proof that readers do want to know what happens between the sheets.

What else do I like about these books?

The authors publish often and they are accessible to their readers.

If you find a favorite author, make sure to write to her and look her up on social media. She will probably write you back and she will likely even have a Facebook group for you to join so that you can find out more about her, her new releases, and about any giveaways she's having.

The book that I'm currently re-reading for what feels like the tenth time is Charlotte Byrd's *Lavish Lies,* which used to be called House of York. It's a trilogy about a girl who is kidnapped and forced to participate in a Bachelor-like competition for the hand of the King. The setting is present-day but with a twist. There is no international cabal that trades women like property and controls the world, right? Or is there? I hope you get that I'm being sarcastic.

Charlotte Byrd is probably one of my favorite authors, not just indie but of all time.

I love how simple her language is and

I love how fast the story progresses. I also like her wicked sense of humor.

Someone once left her a bad review that said she writes like "Hemingway and Dr. Seuss with sex" and she took it as one of the biggest compliments she ever received.

In one of her blogs, she wrote, "The point of language is to convey exactly what you mean to keep the story going and that's exactly what I aim to do with each of my sentences."

I spend the morning consumed in a book with other people's problems, and once I read the last page, I feel better about my own.

Reading gives me perspective on my own life.

Nothing that I'm going through is as difficult as what I just read and it's a nice escape into a reality that's not my own.

Unfortunately, it doesn't last long.

## 15

## OLIVE

### WHEN I GET HIM A PRESENT...

Owen returns from his appointment with his parole officer with an eagerness to get back to our previous conversation.

Given that I just spent a few hours trying to cleanse myself of it, I refuse to engage.

I try to change the conversation to something more palatable but whatever we talked about before just doesn't click.

Our sentences don't connect well to each other and the pauses are big enough for trucks to drive through.

We eat lunch in silence with only the television flickering in the background.

After we do the dishes, finally an interesting topic of conversation arises.

After years in prison, Owen isn't exactly up to date on any technological advancements. The few cell phones that people have managed to sneak behind bars are old and have limited functionality.

I show him what my phone can do and he examines it as if it were a bomb. He is afraid to press any button out of fear of making it blow up.

"You know, nothing is going to happen," I say over and over again but it doesn't seem to register.

"What if I push this?" he asks my permission for each command.

"Yeah, you can do that," I say with a nod.

As he plays around with it more and more, he finally starts to relax.

I show him how to go on to YouTube and how to read the news.

Then I show him how to set up a private email account (he needs one that's not monitored by the Department of

Corrections) and some social media profiles. He immediately wants to look up his old friends and smiles from ear to ear when he is able to scroll through their pictures going back years.

"Okay, if you're going to do this, you're going to have to get your own phone," I say.

The T-Mobile store isn't crowded and an associate sees us right away.

I help Owen pick out his phone, trying to explain the differences between Android and Apple operating systems even though I hardly know a thing about Androids.

He examines each available phone carefully while I wait and start the next book in the *Lavish* trilogy on mine.

A text appears on the screen.

*We have a job tonight. You free?*

Given that I'm no longer employed and I don't really want to spend the evening fighting about him with Owen, I would say that my schedule is wide open.

*Pick you up at seven,* Nicholas texts.

Owen finally decides on the iPhone,

the latest model and we go through the motions of adding him to my plan.

"I'm going to pay you back as soon as I get a job," Owen promises.

"It's no problem, really," I say. "It's not like you rack up any minutes or anything like you could years ago."

"What do you mean?" he asks and I explain the limitations of phone plans past.

When I'm signing the receipt, my phone dings again.

It's laying right next to me on the counter and Owen leans over and reads the message.

"Wear something nice," he says. "You going out tonight?"

I nod and thank the associate for his time.

I start to walk toward the front door, but Owen doesn't follow me.

He just stands there next to the cash register, as if he is frozen in space. I wave him over but he still doesn't budge.

"You're going out with *him* again?" he asks.

He doesn't even try to lower his
voice.

"Yes, I am," I whisper loudly. "And it's
none of your business."

Three teenagers pile into the store
speaking loudly and laughing. For a
second, I hesitate and debate whether I
go should back there and try to physically
escort him out.

That will just make a scene.

Instead, I open the door and walk
outside. A few moments later, Owen is
right next to me.

"You can't go out with him," he says,
grabbing my arm.

"You know what? I've had enough. I
will date and see whomever I choose. It's
none of your business and you need to
stay out of it."

"You're my sister, Olive. I love you."

The word *love* cuts me like a razor
blade.

I didn't grow up in a family where
people ever used it and I've never said it
to anyone before either.

I don't know if Owen is telling me the

truth, but it sort of feels like a pile of garbage.

"You don't mean it," I say. "Stop saying things you don't mean."

"Don't tell me how I do or don't feel. I do *love* you. That's why I'm so upset about this."

I take a deep breath and walk toward the car. He follows me down the parking lot.

"I know you two have a past," I say and then I have a lightbulb moment. Maybe if I were to pretend that I knew more than I knew he would actually tell me the truth.

"Nicholas told me everything..." I start to say before he interrupts me.

"What did he tell you?"

"Everything," I say, looking him straight in the eye.

It's a bluff but he can't know it's a bluff if I want him to believe it.

I am no stranger to lying but this is the first time I've ever lied to my brother and it makes me feel dirty.

Still, there are things you must do to get what you want.

"Whatever he told you is a fuckin' lie, Olive."

I shrug and get into the car. I start the engine but don't move it from park. I want to give this my full attention.

"What did he say?" He prods me but I seal my lips. "Okay, well, if you don't tell me what he told you, I'll just tell you what he did."

I nod and wait.

"He told you that this whole thing is about Nina, right? That girl I was seeing who he slept with? Well, it's not."

I keep my face as stoic and expressionless as possible.

So, this whole thing, this whole beef is just about a girl?

Of course, wars have been started over women so it's not exactly a little thing.

"I loved her, Olive. We were going to be together. We had our whole life planned. And then he just swooped in and acted all arrogant and cavalier, just like he is acting with you...and she...she told me she didn't care about him but then she slept with him."

"When did this happen?"

"Two days before the shooting."

"Oh, shit," I whisper. "I'm really sorry," I add, putting my arm around him.

He is trying to hide it but there are tears bubbling up to the surface. He puts his head in his hands and turns away from me.

Now, I get it. Now, I understand why this is still affecting him so much.

If he had been on the outside then he would probably not even remember her name now. She would've been just an old girlfriend who cheated on him and who wasn't worth his time.

But time stopped for him when he went into prison.

That is his last memory of his life on the outside and no matter what he does he can't wipe it clean.

"But, Owen, this was years ago. I mean, that was a really shitty thing to do but...I can't stop seeing him just because of that."

He slowly lifts up his head. His eyes focus on mine, no longer ashamed of the tears.

"That's what he told you, right?" he asks. I nod.

"What about the rest?" he challenges me.

I shrug.

"What about her ending up dead?" he asks.

I inhale and my breath gets lodged in the back of my throat.

"Oh, I see," Owen says with his lips forming into a smile. "He didn't mention that, huh? Her body was found in Connecticut. He was the last person to be seen with her, but he had an alibi and the police could never quite get enough evidence to bring charges."

## 16

## OLIVE
### WHEN I SEE HIM AGAIN...

Later that afternoon, Owen's story hangs in the air above my head as I get ready. I try to cancel but Nicholas texts back that it's impossible.

When we talk on the phone, he makes it clear that if I back out then the deal is off.

It's not so much a threat but a statement.

After sharing the story with me, Owen spends the day playing with his new phone. He doesn't push me any harder and he doesn't mention another word about it.

Climbing into Nicholas' Mercedes, I am consumed by a sense of dread.

He gives me a kiss on the cheek and cold shivers run down my body.

How much of what Owen told me is true?

His tears were spot on and nothing about it felt like a lie.

But then again, I have a lot of experience lying and that's the whole freaking point to it.

"Are you okay?" Nicholas asks. "You seem...off."

I shrug. "I told you, I wasn't feeling well."

"Yeah, I know but I really can't cancel this meeting."

I want to ask him about it. I want to know what I'm getting myself into. I need to know everything I can in order to play a part well. But I can't even bring myself to pose the questions.

"Tell me about Nina," I say instead.

The words just slip out of me without my consent but once they are out I don't regret them.

"Nina was Owen's girlfriend," Nicholas says with a sigh. He has been dreading this conversation but he is not surprised by it. "It was stupid. We met a few times. We flirted and then one night...we slept together."

"Did you know that they were a couple?" I ask.

He doesn't respond for a moment but then gives a slight nod.

"Nina and I ran into each other at a bar. We were friends. They had a fight about him flirting with this other girl. She was jealous. She had a few drinks and she started to play with my hair. I liked her. My girlfriend had just dumped me and I liked the attention," he says, stopping at the red light.

"Go on," I say.

"We had more drinks and then I told her that she couldn't drive home. I didn't want to drive either and there was a motel right next door. I offered that we split the cost of the stay. When we got there...I kissed her. She kissed me back and we ended up spending the night together."

I take a deep breath. This story I can handle, but not what is going to happen next.

"And then?" I prod. "What happened *then*, Nicholas?"

I turn my body toward him and wait for the answer. His eyes remain fixed on the road as he shrugs his shoulders.

"I didn't hear from her for a while. We both had regrets in the morning and we promised each other that we would never tell anyone what happened."

"And then?" I ask again.

He bites his lower lip, finally sliding his eyes toward mine.

"What happened to Nina, Nicholas?" I demand to know. He takes a deep breath. I grab onto the arm rest as if I'm bracing myself for impact.

"She was killed," he says slowly as if uttering the words are causing him pain. "Someone murdered her. They found her body in Connecticut. She had been shot."

I shake my head and look away from him even though I don't want to.

"Did you... shoot her?" I ask quietly.

The car comes to a sudden stop as he pulls into a parking spot on the side of the road.

"Is that what Owen told you?" Nicholas asks. His eyes are bloodshot and full of anger. "Is that what he said? He said I *killed* her?"

When I give him a nod, he grabs onto the steering wheel and shakes it so hard that the whole car quakes.

"I didn't kill her, Olive. She was my friend and we had a good night together. I wanted to see her again but she wanted to make things right with Owen. I gave her the space to do that."

"So what happened to her then?" I whisper.

"I don't know." Nicholas shrugs. "I wish I knew. The cops came to see me. They took my DNA and they confirmed that we did have sex. But that was it. That was all. I had an alibi for that night when they think it happened."

I narrow my eyes.

"I was at the movies. They have me on camera. That's why I'm not in prison right now. That's why the case is still open."

I stare out of the window and at the guys standing at the corner pointing and laughing about their sneakers. I can't hear what they're saying due to the sound of blood pounding through the veins in my head.

"What else do you want to know?" Nicholas asks. "Anything. I didn't do this, Olive. I was an asshole and a cheater but I never hurt her."

He keeps talking trying to get me to believe him. The words come into one ear and out the other.

He talks for some time and then he stops. We sit in silence as I try to figure out who to believe.

---

WE ARRIVE at the restaurant with everything that had just transpired between us still there. He wants me to believe him and I want to as well but wanting and believing aren't the same thing. Owen wants me to believe him, too, and a part of me does.

So, what now?

Can I really go through with this? Play this part?

Pretend like everything is fine when it's anything but? That's my job and I intend to do it well.

When we get to the table, Nicholas introduces me as Abby and himself as Henry. The couple smiles and shakes our hands and makes space for us in their booth.

The place isn't very formal, more like business casual and it's filled with people in their work clothes blowing off some steam.

"So, what do you do, Kristen?" I ask.

She pushes her thick dark hair from her neck and launches into a vivid description of her job at a biomedical lab.

She develops medical devices as does her husband who works on the business end of the company.

"That's where we met," she says in her

thick southern accent. "We both grew up in South Carolina but we ended up meeting here at LinoTech's company picnic. Can you believe that?"

I smile and ask her more about themselves and their jobs.

They are eager to share and I'm eager to listen.

It gives me a chance to think about things without looking like I'm not paying attention.

Occasionally, I nod my head and ask follow-up questions that start them down another alley of conversation.

When the food arrives, Kristen asks us what we do, first looking at Nicholas.

"Real estate," he says. "Pretty boring commercial loan approvals and other finance stuff."

"And you?" Becker asks, giving me a smile.

"I write test questions, for the common core. Math," I say, using the stock answer that Nicholas doesn't want me to delineate from.

This is what I used to do for a living and I share some of the details of what that entails.

For some reason, people tend to find my work fascinating even though they would never want to do it in a million years.

Perhaps, it has something to do with the fact that we have all gone to high school and either suffered or enjoyed our time in math class.

We get another round of drinks and Kristen and I don't pass up the opportunity for a taste of chocolate lava cake.

The waiter comes back with two forks, but Kristen quickly asks him to bring us two more, saying that there's no way that Becker will pass up this indulgence.

"I can't believe I'm having this," I say, taking a bite.

"Mmmm, isn't it good?" she asks.

"Out of this world."

"I can eat three times a day," she adds,

licking the fork in a rather sensual manner.

I watch her as she licks her lips and then brings her fork to Becker's lips. I was wondering when we would get to this portion of the evening.

## 17

## OLIVE

### WHEN HE TELLS ME ABOUT THEM...

We have spent almost two hours talking to them but we have yet to bring up the real reason we are all meeting. Kristen and Becker have something that Nicholas needs and one of the things that they like to do is swing with other couples.

I bring the fork to my lips and watch Becker watching me very carefully. He wants me and I would be lying if I said that a part of me didn't want him as well.

I want to say something but I'm not sure how to bring it up. I may never have been on a first date like this before, but I have been on a first date so I know that in order for it to go well you really have to play it by ear.

On a first date, you are feeling out the other person. You are getting a sense of who he, she, or in this case, they are, in order to figure out if you are a good fit. From the way that Kristen smiles at me and runs her finger up my thigh I get the feeling that this date is mine to fuck up.

Nicholas didn't tell me much about what was going to happen.

All I know is that this couple is looking for another to have a good time with.

I don't know how I feel about that because I don't really know how I feel about Nicholas right now.

Everything that I heard about Nina is making it difficult for me to make rational choices.

Is dating a couple even a rational choice?

I try to ignore the fact that I have never been with a woman let alone two other people in any sexual manner whatsoever.

I know that it's fashionable among many college girls to hook up with girls and threesomes aren't exactly uncommon things on university campuses.

In fact, I think there are more people having threesomes than there are in steady, committed relationships. But I never did anything like that.

I glance over at Becker. His eyes are entirely focused on Kristen, watching her lick her fork.

I'm suddenly in a movie. I'm watching myself watch them. It's an out of body experience because they are so connected to each other and I'm the outsider.

She grazes my leg and suddenly I'm not a foreigner anymore.

I belong.

They want me.

The question is am I down to party?

My hands get clammy as cold sweat originates in my armpit and runs down my arm. Whatever I say, I have to do it very delicately.

I pry my fingers away from the vinyl

seating and place them carefully on her leg. Kristen smiles and licks her lower lip.

Becker and Nicholas are talking somewhere in the distance and with each passing moment their voices get further and further away. I slide over closer to her.

"Wasn't that delicious?" I ask.

She nods her head, tilting it to one side.

"I've never had anything that good before."

"Me either."

"I think I want some more," she whispers after a moment.

I place my palm on top of her thigh and she closes her eyes slowly enjoying the moment.

"I do, too, but maybe not tonight," I say. Her eyes click open. I give her a smile.

"I like you," I whisper. "But...not tonight."

She looks at me confused and then gives me a knowing nod.

"You're not going to ghost me, are you?" she whispers. "You could just tell me that you had a good time but it's not going to work out. I'm totally fine with that."

The waiter comes around with our check, which the men fight to pay for. Finally, Becker caves but insists that Nicholas give him his Venmo email so that he can pay for their share.

"Did you hear what I said?" Kristen whispers. "I get it. It's totally fine."

I look down at the table and then slowly back at her.

My lips part and my tongue rushes to the roof of my mouth. I pick at a little cut in the wood in front of me before explaining.

"It's just that...I've never done anything like this before."

"Really?" she gasps.

I shrug, embarrassed.

"Well, if that's all you're worried about then you don't have to worry about it at all," she says. "No pressure, okay?"

I nod and grin from ear to ear.

"Let's plan to do this again tomorrow

night," I suggest as we all rise from the table.

Kristen smiles but Becker and Nicholas look a little disappointed. She tugs on Becker's sleeve and mouths, "I'll explain it later," into his ear.

When we get back to the car, Nicholas demands an explanation.

"You said you were up for anything."

"I thought I was, but this was a bit too much."

"I didn't need to invite you. I could've done it myself."

"They were into that?"

"Probably. I'm quite charming."

I roll my eyes. We are arguing about the job, but we both know that this isn't what's on our minds at all. There's something bigger going on.

"I wasn't ready," I finally admit. "I thought I might be when you told me but after what you said about Nina, I just didn't feel...aroused."

He clenches his jaw.

"I don't know how far this will need to go," he says. "I just need them to be comfortable with us. She has the USB drive in her purse along with her computer. From what my sources say, it's attached to her laptop. It has to be for proprietary reasons. She carries it around everywhere and that's why I need them both to relax and get comfortable to make the switch."

"But why can't you just break into their apartment or something like that?" I ask.

"The security is on the level of the Pentagon. She is a very high-level person at the company. That's why they take all of these precautions. But they have a weakness, a fatal flaw if you may. They like to party."

I wait for him to continue but he stops. I stare at him. Our eyes meet.

"You should have warned me that you were going to put a stop to this," he says.

"Are you angry?"

He shrugs and looks away.

"I have to be able to rely on you. If I can't, then this isn't going to work."

The valet pulls up with his car and he

gives him a generous tip. We climb in and drive silently for a few minutes.

"This is a big step for me," I say. "I've never done anything like this before and I wasn't sure how it was going to go."

"You've been to the swinger club in Hawaii. You even found your friend there," he says, smiling out of the corner of his lips.

I shake my head in disappointment. He thinks this is funny, when it's anything but that.

"I'm sorry," he apologizes but it doesn't feel like enough.

"I don't want you to do anything you don't want to do," he says. "But this is my only way in. They don't trust me. They are very cautions. We can't just befriend them. But they like to have sex with strangers."

"I left things on a positive note," I say. "I didn't ruin anything."

"But if you're not into this then it won't do me any good."

## 18

## OLIVE

### WHEN THINGS TAKE A TURN ...

I shake my head and fold my arms across my chest.

Is he serious? Is he really trying to convince me to do something I don't want to do?

Anger starts to bubble to the surface and I can't control it.

"You have no right to do this," I say in a raised tone. "You just asked me to be your girlfriend and now you want me to have sex with some couple that we just met. I've never even kissed a girl before."

"You haven't?" He is taken aback.

I roll my eyes.

"I'm sorry, I didn't mean it the way it

came out. I'm just...surprised. I mean, I thought nowadays everyone sort of fooled around with...everyone."

"If you thought that then why did you ask me be to exclusive?"

He slows down at a red light and turns to look me straight in the eye. Reaching out, he runs his finger down my jaw as if he is outlining it.

"I want you to be my girlfriend," he says after a moment. "I do. And this has nothing to do with that."

I shrug my shoulders.

"This is just a job. You said yourself that you wanted to fuck Dallas, right. Remember him?"

"Dallas was different. I just met him. He was hot. We were alone. It was something I've done before."

I expect him to come at me again, to try to convince me. But much to my surprise, he doesn't.

He just says that I don't have to do anything I don't want to do.

We drive all the way back to his hotel room in silence. If he has an apartment somewhere here, it's a mystery to me. But I'm not interested in staying over. I have a headache and I'm tired of the games.

"Take me home," I say, when he pulls up to the curb of his hotel.

He takes a moment to register his surprise before pulling away.

It's only when we get to the end of the corner that I realize that I might have made a mistake.

It's not that I don't want to stay the night at his place, it's that I want him to make me. Not really force me in that way where it's against my will. But rather just insist that I do it. Then I'll know that he cares.

"I don't want you to do anything you don't want to do," Nicholas says, pulling up to the curb near my apartment building. "If this is too much for you, I totally understand."

"So, how are you going to get it?"

"I won't," he says, putting the car in park. I narrow my eyes.

"So, what then?"

He shrugs. "I don't know, but I have to devise another plan. If it's possible."

"Why do you need this flash drive?" I ask.

He swallows hard but does not answer. I ask again and again he doesn't respond.

"It's a job, Olive. The less that you know about it, the better," he finally says.

"I don't think that's true," I insist. "I can do anything if I have to, but if I don't understand why then I have a hard time making myself commit to something."

He sits back in the seat and runs his index finger along the seam of the steering wheel.

He's thinking.

Analyzing.

Trying to figure out how much he should tell me.

At the end, he says nothing.

"This is just one thing I cannot tell you. You either do this or you don't. But don't do me any favors."

I fold my leg under my butt and turn to face him.

"What's going to happen in their hotel room if we go there?" I ask. He shrugs.

"I don't know. You told her that you weren't that experienced, so maybe nothing. Or maybe everything."

"What if I say I don't want to. That I won't do it?" I ask, my voice cracks in the middle of the question.

This is the first time I have verbalized how I really felt.

Nicholas turns to face me. "I am not going to make you do anything you don't want to do, Olive. I can't tell you anymore about this job than I already did. It's not safe."

"What's going to happen to us, if I don't do it?" I ask.

"I still want to be with you," he says after a moment.

"Do you still want to be my partner?" I ask.

He turns away from me. I ask again but he refuses to give me an answer. When I get out of the car and walk into my building, I know that the offer is no longer valid.

WHEN I GET HOME, I try to tiptoe past Owen on the couch who turns around and catches me in the act. I let out a loud groan and tell him that I'm in no mood for an argument. He tosses his hands up in the air and buries his head in his paperback.

I slip out of the uncomfortable pantyhose and bra and drop the rest of the clothes on the floor.

I head straight into the shower to wash the fight off me. I prefer to shower at night and go to bed clean but tonight I don't feel particularly fresh.

People don't like to admit it but couples who date other couples and go to bed with them is not that uncommon of an activity. The thing is that few people talk about it.

It's not the physical that takes me aback though.

Kristen and Becker are both quite attractive and with a little bit of alcohol, I can see how this could be an interesting way to pass the time.

So, what is it that's bothering me?

I don't quite know.

Nicholas was right.

When I saw Dallas, I wanted to sleep with him.

He oozed sexuality and I wanted to feel his hands all over me.

Perhaps what's different now is the date itself.

Maybe it's just being too much in my own head.

When I went over to see Dallas, my attraction to him just took over.

I felt myself being swept away and we could have had a really good time if we hadn't been interrupted.

I felt the same way when we went to that club in Hawaii.

All of those hot couples around us touching and kissing, who wouldn't want to join in? But there was another interruption.

But meeting Kristen and Becker with

the explicit intention of feeling them out just puts me too much in my own head.

I can't let my body take over.

I can't lose myself in the moment.

And now? What happens now exactly? If I can't do this job, then are we done? At least, professionally speaking that is.

And if so, then what happens to *me*?

Tears start to well up in the back of my eyes.

I bury my face in my hands. I just feel so impotent and so stupid.

I had quit my job.

My well-paying, important job with a career trajectory for a man.

Just a guy.

Yes, he's hot and he's good with his hands and he knows his way around my body but so what? I should have known better.

I shouldn't have been so impulsive.

Only men do this.

Only men risk everything in the world for one moment of pleasure and I am not a man.

I should have been above this.

I don't hear him come in until he takes a seat right next to me on the bed.

He doesn't ask me questions. He just puts his arm around my shoulder and just holds me.

I sob loudly and try to wipe my eyes over and over again.

## 19

## OLIVE
### WHEN I TALK TOO MUCH...

"I don't think we're going to work together anymore," I say.

He doesn't know much about the offer that Nicholas made to me and I should keep my mouth closed about it but the words just spill out.

Owen just nods and listens, holding me tightly.

I have missed this closeness even though it feels foreign.

We were never close growing up, in fact we fought more than we played.

But now that I'm grown, it's nice to have someone who is family to care about me.

My vision is blurry along with my memory, and I can't remember exactly what I told Owen about what happened in Hawaii before.

I know that I tried to cover for him but tonight I don't.

"So, that's why you quit your job?" he asks. "Because he was going to pay you a million dollars to work with him?"

I nod.

"And what is it that you're going to do together?"

I shrug my shoulders but keep my head propped against him.

"Olive, answer me." He shrugs me off.

Suddenly, I realize my mistake.

I have given him ammunition that I should not.

I had confused his caring actions toward me as someone who might just listen to my problems and not try to shove his opinion down my throat.

"I shouldn't have said anything," I say, pulling my bathrobe tight.

"How could you be so stupid?" he

says, standing up. "How could you agree to something this ridiculous? How could you give up a nice paying job that you worked really hard to get for that?"

I take a deep breath in an effort to calm the anger that feels like it is just below the surface, ready to erupt at any moment.

"What is even on that flash drive?" He demands to know. "What if it's something top secret? What if it's something that's classified? What if you are doing something that can put you away in prison for many years?"

He's right.

Of course, he's right.

I should know these things.

I need to know what I'm walking into. It's one thing to steal jewelry and things like that but it's a whole other thing to take corporate and government secrets.

Of course, I can't admit that to him, not now and probably not ever.

I don't say anything for a while but that doesn't stop him from going on a rant and I regret that I ever opened up to him in the first place.

Doesn't he understand that this isn't pulling us close together?

Doesn't he understand that this is only making me want to be with Nicholas again?

At least, he's not here making me choose between my only real family member and the man I love.

There it is.

Love.

That word.

That foreign word that I had never said to anyone before.

Actually, I've never even thought it.

My first high school boyfriend? The reason we broke up was that I couldn't bring myself to say it back to him.

His parents had been married for twenty years and they said it to each other all the time.

That was just the kind of home that he was raised in.

My home?

Whenever my mother said the word 'love' she always used it as a weapon. It either came with a guilt trip or...no, wait, it was just a guilt trip.

She only said it when she wanted me to do something and it was always used in a question.

Don't you know that I love you?

Don't you know that the only reason I'm asking you to do this is because I love you?

"How do you even know that he has any money?" Owen asks, breaking my concentration.

Finally, I have a way to defend Nicholas.

"He paid for my first class tickets to Hawaii. I saw his house," I say.

"It could have just been a rented Airbnb," Owen says smugly.

"I went to a party there. People knew him. He has had that house for a while."

This seems to shut him up but only temporarily.

When he launches into yet another

attack about how dangerous it is to agree to be his partner without knowing a thing about it, I get up and kick him out of my room.

"This conversation isn't over," Owen threatens. "I want to talk about this."

"Well, I don't," I say, and shut the door in his face.

WHEN I WAKE UP, the sun is already high in the sky. I pick up my phone, expecting to see a good morning text from Nicholas. He has sent one for the last few days but this morning there is nothing.

I bite my lower lip and I try to fall back asleep. I scroll aimlessly through Facebook and Instagram and when that gets boring, I read the news.

An hour passes and now I really have to pee. Finally, I force myself out of bed and wash my face.

I put on the most comfortable clothing I can find, basically pajamas and go out in the living room. Much to my surprise, Owen isn't there. I look at the time. It's almost eleven. I try to remember when he said he had to report to his parole officer but nothing comes to mind.

Whatever it is, I enjoy being alone in my apartment again.

As far as I know, Sydney is still in Hawaii even though I haven't heard much from her either. I open the cabinet right next to the microwave and grab the box of Earl Grey tea. Usually, I drink mint but this morning I hope that the caffeine will free me of this terrible headache.

But the box is empty.

"Shit," I say under my breath, shaking my head.

The coffee is also gone. "Shit, shit."

I slip into my boots and grab my coat. There's a coffee shop right around the corner but it will require me to go outside looking like I just woke up.

I glance at myself in the mirror in the foyer.

My hair looks like a bird's nest.

My skin is pale and splotchy around my nose.

My eyes are bloodshot.

My only hope is that I don't run into anyone I know on the way there.

## 20

# OLIVE

## WHEN I HAVE TO MAKE A CHOICE...

While standing in line, I scan the display stand and my mouth waters for the chocolate eclair with pink sprinkles.

It's just junk food, I say to myself. You don't really want it. You're going to regret it as soon as you eat it and you're going to be kicking yourself for it the rest of the day.

"That looks delicious, doesn't it?" the woman standing behind me says.

Her long hair is tied up in a bun and her yoga mat is attached to a strap that swings off her shoulder.

"Yes," I say. "My mouth is watering just looking at it."

"Oh my God, me, too!" she whispers.

She gazes at the eclair as if it were a long lost boyfriend who got away.

If size zero didn't exist before this is the person who it has been invented for.

"You should get it," I say. "I mean, one of us should."

"No, I can't." She laughs. "I didn't just sweat my ass off for an hour and a half to waste it all on that. Why don't you get it?"

I shrug. "I want to, believe me. But I didn't even bother with exercise today. Or in the last decade."

"Okay, so let's be strong together," she suggests and I concur.

When it's my turn to order, I get a tall Earl Grey hot tea and that's it. The barista hands me the cup and I make a fist with my hand in solidarity.

"You can do it," I whisper when I see her hesitating.

We meet up again at the sugar and cream station.

"I didn't get it," the woman announces proudly. "I stayed strong."

"I'm glad."

"I don't think I could've done it without you," she admits, nudging me slightly with her hip.

I smile at her.

On the outside, she looks so well-put together that I never suspected that she might be struggling with the exact same things as I am.

So much for judging the book by its cover, huh?

She is headed to a boutique right near my house so we walk together talking about how crappy the weather has been recently.

"Hey, listen," she says, taking me by the arm and then shoving me into the alley right before my house.

"What are you... doing?" I start to ask before realizing that she has pressed me against the wall and has her index finger in my face.

"Your boyfriend, Nicholas Crawford,"

she says in a completely different tone of voice. "He is in trouble."

"What...how...?" I push her away while I try to understand what is going on but she doesn't budge.

"He owes my boss a lot of money over that Martha's Vineyard job."

"I don't know anything about that."

"You will. You ask him about that. You ask him what he did with that Harry Winston necklace. You ask him what he did to his partner."

I make my hands into fists, readying myself for a fight that I don't think I would win.

"How do you know this?" I mumble, trying to think of something coherent to ask.

"Everyone knows that he's back in town. He's not even trying to hide this fact. And he can't just walk around acting like he didn't steal two million dollars from us when *everyone* knows that he did."

I shake my head. She takes a step away from me and I let out a sigh of relief.

"What do you want me to do about this?" I ask.

She takes a step back, folding her arms across her chest. "Nicholas Crawford doesn't have any money," she says. "What he does have is a certain set of skills."

Her words 'he doesn't have any money' reverberate in my mind like an echo. I hear them over and over again because they confirm my worst fears.

"Are you listening to me? You have to hear what I'm saying, Olive."

I snap my head back. Our eyes meet and I wait.

"That job he refused to do last night, we need that flash drive. And you are going to help him get it," she says.

My mouth drops open.

"You know about that?" I ask.

"He thinks that job was optional and as long as he was willing to do it, we were letting him think that. But it's not and the sooner that he gets that through his head the better it will be for everyone."

I lean back against the wall trying to

gather my thoughts and say something intelligent. But nothing comes to mind.

"I'm going to be frank with you, Olive," she says, getting very close to me as a couple of loud twenty-somethings walk past us on the street. "If we don't have the flash drive by tomorrow morning, then that bounty on Owen's head will be paid."

My ears start to buzz as all the blood rushes to my head.

"What are you talking about?" I whisper.

She starts to walk away and I yell after her again.

She only answers when I catch up to her.

"There's word on the streets that someone wants Owen dead and they're willing to pay one hundred thousand dollars for it. Well, if you don't get us that flash drive, we're going to make it happen."

"I don't know what you're talking about," I say when she starts to walk away again. "I don't know anything about this."

"I think you do," she says. She reaches over to me and presses something into my chest. I flinch worried that it's a weapon but she just laughs and disappears around the corner.

On the ground, I find a scrap of paper with a number and the name Janet Bailey on it.

## 21

## OLIVE

### WHEN I HAVE TO MAKE A CHOICE...

I lean against the wall and stand here for a while. The world should be spinning out of control, but for some reason it isn't.

Instead, my mind focuses entirely on the details. The bricks feel rough against my palms.

The alley has a dewy smell that I hadn't noticed before. The air itself is thick with moisture. Even though it's unpleasant here, I can't make myself go out.

The world is too bright and loud out there. It's also too fast. No, here I am safe.

But a man dressed in a leather jacket

with its collar popped turns off the street
and starts to walk toward me. He takes
out a cigarette and asks me for a light. A
pang of fear shocks me out of my daze. I
quickly tell him that I don't have one and
scurry back out to the street.

I am not sure where to go or what to
do. How much of what Janet said is true I
do not know.

I doubt that's her real name, for one.
But what about the rest?

I know that Nicholas took that
necklace and I know that his partner
ended up dead.

I didn't want to believe Owen when
he said that it was Nicholas who did it but
Janet seemed to all but confirm that.

I know that he had double-crossed his
boss, why wouldn't he double-cross his
partner?

As I walk down the street, getting
further and further away from my home,
I let my feet do the thinking.

I don't know where I am going and
I'm fine with that. What I focus on
instead is another thing that she

mentioned, the part that she thought that I knew.

Nicholas doesn't have any money. Owen suspects that as well but Janet confirmed it.

But what does that mean exactly? And what about his house in Hawaii and all of that first class airfare that he paid for?

Of course, just because he doesn't have millions doesn't mean that he doesn't have any money.

But it does mean that he probably doesn't have the amount that he had promised me.

I only realize where I am when I walk into the lobby of his five-star hotel and head straight to his room. I knock a few times and no one answers. I knock again.

"Sorry, I didn't hear you," he says, clearly surprised to see me. He points to the noise-cancelling headphones around his neck as an explanation.

"Did we talk about meeting up?" he asks, giving me a kiss on the cheek.

"No, I just wanted to come and see you," I say, walking past him.

"I wish you had texted," he says, grabbing the mess of papers off the coffee table.

I wish I hadn't texted so much before, I think to myself. I wish I haven't been such a product of my generation, and always gave warning about where I was and what I was doing.

"Why? Are you hiding something?" I ask, smiling out of the corner of my lips.

"No, of course not," he says, putting his hand around my waist and spinning me around to face him.

When my eyes meet his, a little part of me melts. His fingers graze the outside of my arm, sending shivers down my spine.

My lips part. He licks his.

I feel myself losing control of my body. I raise my hand to his face and touch his mouth.

Our eyes remain locked on each other's and I watch as his pupils enlarge.

"You are so beautiful," he whispers, touching my neck.

My cheeks flush red and I lean away from him, embarrassed by my own embarrassment.

When he touches his lips to mine, I open my mouth and welcome him in.

The longer we kiss the harder it is for me to remember why I had come here in the first place.

It's like my mind becomes blank and the only thing that matters is to touch him and be with him. As my hands move up and down his body, I know that I am not alone in my desire. Nicholas turns off the lights and throws me on the bed.

## 22

OLIVE
WHEN I CHALLENGE HIM...

What the hell did I just do? Lying in his arms, wrapped in about a million-thread count Egyptian cotton sheet, I stare at the ornate ceiling.

How could I do this? I came here to find out if he was lying to me. I came here to get to the bottom of what is going on and I ended up sleeping with him.

My lust for him has no bounds. I don't just want him.

I crave him. I need him.

It's as if I am addicted to him. I have never experienced anything like this before.

The last time we spoke to each other,

we had a fight and yet once I got here, it was as if none of that even mattered.

He took me into his arms and my mind was wiped clean.

I nuzzle myself into his armpit and enjoy the cocoon that he has made for me. This is nice but this can't last.

I have to say something. I have to talk about this. I steel myself for what's to come and when I am finally ready to open my mouth, I hear a loud snore.

I smile and enjoy the excuse to keep lying here. But what is going on with me?

I have never in my life felt like this before. I miss him when he's not around. I want to text and talk to him all the time.

I can never get enough of him. There are important things going on and yet I can barely bring myself to care.

I feel like I've been drugged but I don't want to stop taking it.

Eventually, my eyelids get heavy and I stop fighting the sleep.

With Nicholas' arms firmly around me, I let myself drift off into another world where we can be together and away from all of our problems.

---

A LOUD KNOCK jolts me awake.

Someone yells, "Housekeeping!" through the door and she doesn't hear me yell back, "no, thank you."

The housekeeper starts to wheel in her large cart and only stops when she sees Nicholas, with the sheet held loosely in front of his torso, wave and ask her to come back.

"That was a rude awakening." He laughs, dropping the sheet and jumping back into bed.

He cradles my head with one of his hands and runs his finger along my lower lip with another.

My mouth reaches for his and I slide my hands down his chest.

No, no, no, I keep saying to myself.

It's starting to happen again.

I feel a warm sensation pool in the

core of my body as every cell within me seems to yearn for him.

"No," I say, pushing him away. "We can't do it again."

"And why not?" he asks with a smile, his hand already cupping my breast. "You coming here was a nice surprise."

"That's not why I came."

"Yeah, but it's why you stayed," he says.

Nicholas touches me again but I use all of my energy to not succumb to him.

I know that I wouldn't have the strength to do this if we hadn't fooled around already.

"No, I want to talk to you about something."

He sits back against the headboard. "Ask me anything."

My eyelids start to flicker, blink rapidly, without my control.

I rub the back of my neck as I try to figure out how to start or what to say.

Should I tell him about Janet? I don't know.

"Take your time, it's okay," Nicholas

says, putting his arm around me when my breath quickens. "Whatever you have to say, just say it. It's just me, Olive."

That's what I want to believe as well. It's just Nicholas Crawford. I know him.

We've spent a lot of time together. We shared secrets about our past.

But the thing is that I don't really know anything about him. At least, nothing substantial.

Except of course, that I have this insatiable drive to be with him.

"I was thinking about the offer," I begin. "I know that I made a mistake with Kristen and Becker before and you said that we aren't going to work together anymore..."

"Actually, Kristen texted and she asked if we were free this evening," he interrupts me.

This catches me off guard.

"You don't have to go if you..." he starts to say but it's my turn to interrupt.

"We can talk about that later but what I was wondering was...when are you going to pay me?"

He sits up a little and then slides back down.

This isn't what he was expecting me to say.

"Anytime," he says.

"Really?" I raise my eyebrows. "That's great. Because I have my rent and all of these other bills to pay."

"Yes, of course," he says. "Is a check okay?"

I nod. If he's bluffing then he's really good at it. But what would be the point?

He has to know that I will deposit the check as soon as I can and if there's no money under it then the truth will come out.

"How much do I owe you?" he asks, grabbing the check book from his briefcase.

"It was a million dollars over a year, right?" I ask, taking out my phone. He nods.

"So, you owe me for two weeks. That's thirty-eight thousand, four hundred sixty-one dollars, and fifty-three cents. But you can make it out to thirty-eight thousand if you want."

"Look at you, being generous!" Nicholas says.

After signing the check, he hands it to me and leans back against the wall. It's for the full amount I quoted.

"Thank you," I whisper.

I'm shocked a little, given that I've never held this much money in my hand before.

My fingers and toes start to tingle and I cross and uncross my legs trying to get comfortable.

Okay, calm down and get a hold of yourself.

There might not be any money behind this. Anyone can write a check.

For all you know, it's probably going to bounce.

"And I can deposit it?" I ask. Nicholas stares at me for a long time and then laughs.

"Of course. What, you think I'm going to write you a bad check?"

## 23

## NICHOLAS
### WHEN I LIE...

The check is bad.

At least for the time being. It won't be bad if she waits two more days to deposit it and I get the flash drive to the client.

Right now, I have less than three-thousand dollars to my name. But it's Saturday afternoon and the banks are closing in an hour.

They will remain closed tomorrow and the earliest that she can deposit that money is Monday morning, if she is that enterprising.

The flash drive is worth two-hundred

thousand to me because of how difficult it is for me to get.

And it is worth probably five times that to the client because of the information that it contains.

A wiser person would have never made her promises that he couldn't keep. But I have always been the type to live life at the edge of my seat. I paid off her debt when I still had about half a million left because I wanted her to trust me and I owed my own dead sister my own debt.

Olive is very good at what she does, when she does it. She's cautious and careful and an excellent partner.

I know this because she doesn't like partners and she has always worked alone. I don't know the extent of her experience but from the rumors I heard it is extensive.

And if even ten percent of those rumors are true then it's more than enough to get me back on my feet.

The million dollar offer? Only one part of that isn't true.

I have all intentions of paying the

money as soon as I get my hands on it myself. She'll forgive me for that, right? Let's just hope she doesn't find out.

Olive touches my hand with hers, arresting my train of thought.

In bed, we are like dynamite.

Dangerous.

Difficult to control once ignited.

Explosive.

But what are we on the outside?

How does she feel about me for real?

Asking her to be exclusive with me was one of the hardest things I've ever had to do. It seems like nothing. People do it all the time. They fall in love and tell each other how they feel. Not me. I can joke. I can be fun. I can have a good time. But I cannot tell a woman the depth of what I feel for her. And I definitely, cannot tell this woman.

"Are you okay?" Olive asks. "You got so quiet all of a sudden."

"Just thinking."

"About what?"

"You."

She smiles. She probably wants me to

elaborate, but I don't. She probably thinks I'm acting like this on purpose. Being dark and mysterious. Not because I'm really a coward. Not because I really can't bring myself to say the one thing I really want to.

"So, the money... you have the money, right?" she asks. I nod.

"Why do you ask?"

"I'm sorry, I know that it's private and sort of rude to talk about money."

"It's rude to talk about money?" I ask.

"Isn't it? Isn't that what people say? That it's a low-class thing to do?"

"I think only people who say they have more money than they know what to do with are people who don't want other people, with real problems, to know how good they have it."

This makes her laugh and I let out a small sigh of relief.

"I was just talking to Owen and he put all of these shitty ideas in my head," Olive continues.

I'm tempted to put him down but I take the high road, the long view. I need to become his friend, no matter how impossible that seems, and in order to do that I need Olive.

"How's he...adjusting to everything?" I ask.

"Not well," she admits. "I mean, he went to see his parole officer and he's going to try to find a job soon but we've been fighting a lot."

"Really?"

"He just really hates you. And when we had that fight, I was so angry with you and he was there eager to listen. I was so stupid," she says, burying her head in her hands.

"What happened?" I ask, draping my arm over her shoulder.

"Nothing," she whispers and rubs her temples.

"What happened, Olive?"

She reaches for the bottle on the nightstand, opens it, and takes a sip. The cardboard tag around the head says that it costs five dollars.

"Did he do something to hurt you?" I

ask, putting the price of the water out of my mind.

"No, no, of course not," she says quickly. "It's quite the opposite actually. He's so overprotective of me, I feel like I'm starting to suffocate."

"Why don't you come and stay here?" The words escape my lips just as I realize the mistake that this would be. I don't want to drive a wedge between Olive and Owen, I want her to bring us together.

"No, I can't," she says to my relief. "He just got out of prison and I don't want him to be all alone. I also don't want him to go and stay at our mother's."

"Yeah, that wouldn't be good for anyone."

She nods her head and shakes her foot nervously again. Picking up the check, she runs her fingers over the numbers.

"This means so much to me," she whispers. "I have no idea how I was going to pay my rent without it."

"Your rent isn't that high, I hope," I joke, saying a silent prayer that I can get the flash drive tonight or at the very least she doesn't deposit it right away.

"No, of course not. With this, I'm going to have plenty left over."

I tilt the conversation back to Owen and why he doesn't like me.

I want to know what she knows and she explains a bit leaving out the thing that I am pretty certain that he told her about.

In fact, we have already talked about it. I told her what happened, I am just not sure if I had been convincing enough.

"Did he say anything else about Nina?" I ask, getting tired of going in circles around the one thing that I want to talk about.

"No," she says, shaking her head. "He thinks you did it but we didn't talk about it again."

I give her a nod.

The main reason why befriending Owen is a particularly difficult proposition for me is not because I slept with his girlfriend all of those years ago and he's still pissed at me for it.

No, Owen thinks that she is dead because of me. He thinks that I killed her. And who would want to be friends with someone who murdered their girlfriend?

"Do you think I did it?" I ask, looking up at her trying to glean her answer from her body language rather than from the words coming out of her mouth.

"Would I be here if I did?" she asks.

"I guess you have a point there." I smile.

She lies down next to me and pulls the blankets over her shoulders. "I want to stay here forever," she says. "And never leave."

"I'm not sure I have enough for that," I say. "This suite is a grand and a half a night."

"So, when are we meeting Kristen and Becker tonight?" she asks, giving me a wink.

# 24

## OLIVE
### WHEN I LIE...

I won't be able to deposit Nicholas' check until the banks open on Monday. I could've rushed out of his hotel room right when he gave it to me and run over to the branch a few blocks away but I thought that would look a little bit suspicious.

No, I can wait until Monday. The check is so big that if it clears then I'm certain that he has the money. And if not, this will be more than enough to last me the year.

The thing that I need to worry about now is what's going to happen in about five minutes. Oh, wait, I'm wrong. I don't even have that long.

"Hey! It's so nice to see you again," Kristen says, giving me a peck on the cheek.

We're meeting in the bar of a three-star hotel that they recommended. It's not that cheap but it's not very expensive either. We are upper middle class professionals after all, but that doesn't mean that we have a grand to plop down on some five-star treatment.

Kristen is dressed in a form-fitting red dress, black heels, and a shawl, which she uses to either cover or uncover her shoulders depending on what the mood calls for.

She talks quickly and passionately about the new project that she just started at work as if we are old friends. Most of it goes over my head, partly because I'm only half listening and partly because I'm nervous about what's going to happen tonight.

Instead of letting Kristen grab the seat next to me, Becker takes the one between

me and her instead, making the
arrangement boy-girl instead.

When we've had two rounds of
drinks, my nerves finally start to relax a
bit. I don't bounce my foot so much on
the bottom of the bar stool and I keep my
hands from tapping on the table.

But then Becker launches into a story
about a commercial loan that the guy
couldn't close and knocks over his drink.

"Oh my God, are you alright?" I ask,
nearly launching myself out of my chair
to grab a napkin.

"Yeah, I'm fine." He laughs.

The smile vanishes when I press the
napkin into his crotch to soak up the
alcohol. It only hits me what I'm doing
when I feel it get hard.

Becker smiles at me and licks his lips.
Before I can stop myself, I do the same.

The alcohol has gone to my head but
I can't blame it on just that. It's not an
excuse.

Were I to tell the truth, the alcohol is
giving me permission to do what I really
want to do. I take my hand off my leg and

place it on his thigh. He gives me another smile when I give it a little squeeze.

It is only when I manage to pull my eyes away from him that I realize that both Nicholas and Kristen are staring at us.

"I'm sorry," I whisper quietly.

"Oh, no, don't be," she says, wrapping her arm around Nicholas' shoulder. "I was wondering if you were going to get shy again."

Her words come out like molasses and the accent is incredibly sexy.

"Well, I am shy," I admit.

There's no use in pretending that I am at all experienced in this sort of thing but I hope that my naiveté and innocence makes them feel at ease with me.

"That's okay," Kristen says, parting her lips. Nicholas leans closer to her and kisses her on the cheek.

"I'm not," he whispers into her ear.

The conversation at the bar continues well into our appetizer course even though none of us are particularly into it.

When we talk about our work, the

others ask mundane questions that no one really wants any answers to.

As I nurse my third vodka tonic, I get the sense that we are all waiting for something to happen only no one is actually starting the ignition.

"Why don't we take our drinks upstairs?" I suggest.

---

THE HOTEL ROOM is much bigger than I thought it would be. It's actually a suite with a separate bedroom and living room. It's appointed in contemporary mid-century modern style furniture and there is neutral yet uplifting artwork on the walls. Everything is a shade of gray, some darker and some lighter in tone.

Becker and Kristen have been here before because her large tote bag sits underneath the table at the far end. I had looked for this bag, which Nicholas said never left her side at the bar, hoping that we could make the switch there or perhaps even in the bathroom if she had joined me there but, unfortunately, she left it up here.

Becker opens the mini-bar and offers us another round. I opt for a single-serving bottle of white wine and take a seat on the couch, not far from the three of them. When their backs are turned I take a quick peek inside the bag.

The flash drive is attached to the laptop via some sort of metal cord, the exact replica of which Nicholas gave me. In fact, we both have one. We also both have a pair of small pliers with which to cut the original cord so that we can make the switch to the dummy flash drive.

Switching it for a dummy drive is more complicated than just swiping it but it will buy us a lot more time in the end. Who knows how long Kristen will go without using that flash drive again.

If luck is on our side then she won't access it until Monday.

In one and a half days, she will take it with her to brunch (they have a standing Sunday morning reservation at a French cafe that serves the most delicious crepes).

Then maybe she'll take in a matinee and do who knows what else before going back to her apartment.

By the time she discovers that her flash drive has been compromised, we will be long gone.

Besides, she would have come in contact with so many other people that she might not suspect us at all.

"And when she delivers the bad news to her boss," Nicholas pointed out earlier that afternoon, "she will forget to bring up the sexy couple that they spent Saturday night with out of fear of being outed as someone who does this sort of thing."

"I hate that this is something that people still can't talk about," I said. "I hate that we can use it as a weapon."

"Yes, me, too, but in this game, we must use whatever weapon we have access to," Nicholas said.

Moving one of the throw pillows from one side of the couch to another just as

Kristen and Becker turn toward me, I reposition the laptop.

It's a simple illusion, one of the first tricks they teach little kids in magic school. Move something voluminous and, preferably, large with one hand to draw the audience's attention there while quickly doing what it is you mean to do with the other.

Unfortunately, I don't have enough time to switch the flash drives. I will need Nicholas to cause even more of a distraction.

"Oh, let me get that out of your way," Kristen says, grabbing her bag.

Shit.

Does she suspect something?

My heart drops into my stomach but I don't let a single bead of sweat show up on my forehead.

"You mind if I sit down next to you?" Becker asks, taking a seat before I answer.

# 25

## OLIVE
### WHEN I MAKE A MOVE...

It's hard to know whether or not my heart is beating out of my chest because of the job or because of what I am about to do.

What are *we* about to do? I glance over at Becker who brushes his thick auburn hair out of his face, rubbing his chin with his hand.

I've seen this look before in bars where men first make eye contact but before they buy you a drink.

It's the expression of a person asking permission.

Is it okay to talk to you?

Is it okay to offer to buy you a drink?

In Becker's case, he's asking, is it okay to touch you?

Is it okay to fuck you?

If it were any other time, under any other circumstance and it were just me and him, my answer would be yes.

He's smart and he has made me laugh.

He has a quick sense of humor and a sharp tongue, enough to keep me entertained.

And he is not at all hard on the eyes.

But with his wife looking on, I feel shy.

I cower in my seat and turn my whole body somehow inward.

I try to force myself upright but my limbs refuse to cooperate.

"I'm sorry, I just feel a little...off," I finally say.

"Maybe you need another drink?" Kristen suggests.

"I think maybe I had two too many," I joke.

Glancing over at Nicholas, I see the disapproving look, the scowl.

I know what he wants to say without him having to say it.

If you weren't ready, why did you insist on coming? I could've done this myself.

"It's okay, if you don't want to," Kristen says with a disappointed look on her face.

Last night was our first date and anyone can forgive someone for not sleeping with them on the first date.

But tonight? No, this is the only chance I'll get.

I sit back on the couch and uncross my legs.

I take a deep breath.

I take a long look at Kristen and then Becker and finally at Nicholas.

I wait for them to reassure me again that I should be under absolutely no pressure, but luckily none of them do.

They just sip their drinks and wait.

"What about this?" Kristen suggests. "What if you two just kiss...for us...right now?"

Her eyes light up at the idea and so do mine.

Nicholas leans closer to me and touches his lips with mine.

I open my mouth and we move our heads to opposite sides.

His hands grab the back of my neck and press me against the couch. His whole body is leaning into me and it feels both exciting and safe.

At this point, another part of me takes over.

The one that is less cerebral.

The one that doesn't listen to reason but reacts to feelings.

I usually keep this side at bay. I keep it hidden deep inside. But whenever I'm around Nicholas, it emerges. I thought I could only be this way with him in private but the feelings are so powerful they overwhelm my other senses.

Suddenly, there is no Kristen or Becker.

There is only us.

Our hands, our mouths, our bodies. Nicholas' hands are on my breasts and his mouth is on my shoulder.

My lips kiss his neck while my fingers dig into his hair.

When I hear her laughter, I pull away briefly and see that Kristen and Becker are lost in each other's embrace as well.

She is sitting on top of him with her legs straddling his torso.

He pulls up her shirt, leans her back a little bit, and then kisses her stomach.

"I want to see her on all fours," Becker whispers, not really to Nicholas or Kristen or me, just in our general direction.

Kristen's eyes flicker in surprise.

She inhales but doesn't exhale as she waits for my response.

But there is nothing to fear. His words don't scare me. In fact, they just turn me on. Seeing that this is making me hot, Nicholas stands up and gives me the space to flip over.

I lean with my arms on the back of the couch and my knees on the cushions.

Nicholas tugs at the hem of my dress for a few moments before finally rolling it up to my waist, exposing my bare bottom.

He doesn't have much time.

Before we met them, we had agreed that we would have to work quickly. Whichever one of us is the closest to the bag, that's the person who will do it.

And now, with him standing over me, I am glad that we knew that there was no way that we could communicate with anything other than grunts and simple words.

Leaning over me, he touches the outside of my butt cheeks and I flex and relax them.

The air feels thick with electricity and when I glance over at Kristen, I see Becker with his head buried in between her legs.

I dig my fingernail into Nicholas' side. When our eyes meet, I glance over at the laptop. He gives me a slight nod as I let out a loud sigh.

I'm about to flip over on my back, but he stops me, reaching into a tiny pocket in the ruching of my dress and pulling out my pliers.

These are closer to him than his own,

which are held up by his left sock and buried into his shoes.

The pliers disappear up his sleeve as he flips me over onto my back. I reach up to him as my mouth searches for his skin.

As my lips slide down his chest toward his belly button, he snips off the metal cord and slips the flash drive into his pocket.

A few more demonstrative kisses later, and he gives me three taps of his index finger on my collarbone.

That's the sign that the fake flash drive is attached to the laptop. The mission is complete.

He slides back down on top of me, pressing his mouth on mine. It's now safe to pull away. It's now safe to make an excuse and leave.

The relief that sweeps over me is hard to describe. Moments like these are always tense and full of uncertainty and there is still a strong possibility that we could get caught. But for now, we did it.

When he feels me drifting away, Nicholas touches my face.

Our eyes meet and everything else in the room stops existing. There is no more them. There is no more job. There is just us.

It feels dangerous to be with him and I can't stay away. I'm a moth drawn to a flame.

At some point, I'm going to get burned but that's okay. I accept that fate because of what I can experience in the meantime. Perhaps, it's stupid and ill-advised but none of that matters now. Touching him sends shivers through me. I crave his smooth hard body and I want him to do bad things to me.

His skin has a thick masculine smell that intoxicates every part of my being. Every time I inhale, I fall deeper under his spell and I don't ever want to wake up. Nicholas presses his lips into the space between my neck and my collarbone. I bury my hands in his hair and tug a little too hard.

His tongue gives me a lick and I tilt my head back from pleasure. He then runs his tongue up the side of my throat, taking his mouth back to mine.

When our lips find each other again, shocks of electricity rush through me. His tongue moves slowly but mine demands a faster pace. With his jacket off, I tug at his tie and pull it over his head. Then I unbutton his shirt.

He wants to take it easy but I don't want to wait. I flip over onto the couch and press my butt against him. I close my eyes and wait in anticipation as he unbuckles his pants and presses himself to me.

He's hard and big and I tilt my butt higher in the air to welcome him to go further. A moment later, he slips on a condom and thrusts himself inside.

He holds onto my hips as leverage as he slides in and out of me. I put my head on my forearms as my head starts to buzz. His hands make their way up my body to my breasts and play with my nipples.

I tilt my head back with pleasure. He buries his hands in my hair, giving it a little tug with each of his moves. It makes my scalp tingle, sending shivers down my body.

We move back and forth as one until a fire starts to build deep inside of my core. Once it lights, it spreads quickly through me igniting every part with its heat. I tense my feet and point my toes trying to hold on but it bursts out of me with one long moan.

## 26

## OLIVE

### WHEN HE DOESN'T SHOW UP...

I don't know what came over me.

There was nothing planned. In fact, I had planned the exact opposite.

We were going to kiss. We were going to touch each other. Maybe, we were going to get a bit undressed.

But we had a safe word. If I didn't want to go any further then I wouldn't have to. We talked about having a safe word, something I would say if I didn't want to take it much further.

But words like "divine" or "amazing" wouldn't translate well into then having me pull away from what we were just doing. I considered other words. A noun perhaps, like "necklace" or "pomegranate" but those would be difficult to work into the conversation seamlessly.

No, if I had wanted to stop, I could do that by doing just that, stopping.

They knew I was inexperienced in this sort of thing and people without much of a history tend to get shy. I thought that would happen to me. I thought that that part of me that Nicholas seems to unlock and bring to life would shut down.

But after he slid that flash drive into his pocket, I couldn't stop myself. My hands just made their way around his body and there was nothing I could do but let myself go on the ride.

I had only remembered that Kristen and Becker were there at all after it was all done. I lay down on the bed, pulled up the sheets, and let out a big sigh.

"Well, that was...hot," Kristen says. "You two really lost yourselves in each other, huh?"

I nod and smile.

"How was that?" she asks.

"I've never done anything like this before," I say, shrugging.

"Oh, I think you have." Becker laughs.

"You know what I mean."

"How do you feel about it?" Kristen asks.

I look up at the ceiling and think about it.

It's hard to explain. I don't want to be rude, but it was almost as if they weren't there at all.

"It was nice to know that you two were here," I lie. "Maybe next time we can take it to another level."

Kristen and Becker's faces light up.

This is what they have been waiting to hear all this time. After spending a few minutes talking about sports and the weather, I say that we really have to get back home.

We make tentative plans for the following weekend and kiss each other goodbye.

"Won't they get suspicious if we

cancel our next date?" I ask when we walk out of the lobby.

"We don't have to," he says, smiling out of the corner of his lips. I roll my eyes.

"It's not good to mix business and pleasure."

"Yeah, you're right," he says.

"So, what are we going to say about next weekend?"

"Becker is going to get a call on Thursday from me telling him that we broke up. It was too much for you. You're jealous about how much time I spent looking at Kristen and you just can't handle watching me with another woman."

It sounds like a plausible excuse but then something occurs to me.

"Wait a second, why am I the one who is the jealous one here?" I ask. "Why can't it be you?"

"It can," he says, nonchalantly. "But one of us has to make the call and the other one has to be jealous. What do you want to do?"

NICHOLAS WANTS me to sleep over at his place but I want some alone time. Well, not so much alone time as non-hotel room time.

I need to rest and since he can't stay over at my place for obvious brother-related reasons, I leave him at the curb with a little kiss and a promise to text tomorrow.

When I walk through my front door, I expect to see Owen on the couch ready with a lecture as to where I have been. But he's not. He probably just went out with his old friends and lost track of time.

It's Saturday night after all. I decide to draw myself a bath and grab my tablet and my favorite candle. The tub isn't much but it's a tub and it will do.

I have a little stand for my tablet so that I don't accidentally drop it into the water and I stay here until the burning hot water turns lukewarm. Then I head straight into the bedroom, shut the door, and sleep past eleven.

In the morning, Owen is still nowhere to be found. I text him a couple of times, first just saying hello and when he doesn't reply, I get more concerned. The next two texts sound more like demand letters or perhaps outright threats.

WHY AREN'T *you answering your phone?*
*Where the fuck are you?*
*Write me back now!!*

BY THE TIME the sun starts to set, I can't think about anything else. I try to watch TV. I try to look at Facebook and Instagram but nothing holds my interest. And everything reminds me of Owen.

Is he punishing me for going out?

Is he ignoring me on purpose?

Did something happen to him?

We have never lived together as adults. I don't really know if I should expect a courtesy call or text from him, or when.

I didn't tell him much about what I

was doing with my days. Maybe this is his way of getting me back.

Or maybe it's not sinister at all. Maybe he just has the ringer off. He isn't used to carrying his phone around the way we have all become conditioned to do over these last two decades.

Maybe he just left it somewhere and forgot all about it.

All of these maybe's spin around in my head until I start to feel queasy. But no matter how much I try to calm down my nerves with innocent explanations of what might be happening, Janet Bailey's threat keeps coming back to me.

## 27

## NICHOLAS
### WHEN I MEET HIM...

When Olive first insists on coming to meet with Kristen and Becker again, I have my doubts. I don't want to pressure her into doing something she doesn't want to do, especially sexually, but I had to get that flash drive. I wish I knew that Kristen had left the bag in her room before we met up, but I was told she is never apart from it and, unfortunately, I took that intel at face value.

As soon as we got upstairs, I started looking for a way out. The flash drive was attached to the laptop, which was hidden in the bag, which Kristen moved out of the way when she saw Olive inching closer to it. While I turned their attention to the bar, Olive did manage to re-arrange the laptop so that it was pointing the right way up and the metal cord was easy to snip off. But she didn't have enough time to do it.

At first, I expected that I would be working under a ticking clock. How much and how far Olive was willing to go was an unknown to me so my only goal was to make the switch before she asked to slow down. What I didn't expect her to do was to not brake at all.

With the flash drive safe in my pocket, my instinct was to get out of that place. Once the job is done, you should never press your luck by sticking around. But this one wasn't exactly like the others. Even if Kristen were to look into her purse, all they would see is a flash drive attached to the laptop just like she had left it. She would not go through the contents of it now. Why would she?

When I tried to make eye contact with

Olive to see what she wanted to do, I couldn't. Her eyes were closed and her hands were moving their way up and down my body.

I won't lie. It felt good. Good enough to push my luck.

Okay, Olive, I said to myself. If you want this to stop then it's up to you. I will follow your lead but I will not be the leader.

So, that's how it went. I tugged at her clothes and they came off. She pulled at mine and I tossed them away. When the evening came to a close, we'd shared something really special and I'd made two hundred grand, enough to make that bad check I wrote to her go away.

---

"You're late," I say when he grabs the seat next to me.

I know him only as Hawk, which is about as inappropriate as a nickname can get.

He's short, pudgy with a few too many beers around the midsection.

His cheeks flare up easily not just out of embarrassment but also seemingly for no reason whatsoever.

I've only seen him once before. He's the middleman for the guy who hired me, the man whose identity I don't know. When you do what I do, people hear about it and they reach out to you with jobs.

It would be in my best interest to avoid middlemen in the future, but I don't have plans to stay in Boston for long. This is a dangerous place where bad guys want to kill me, the cops want to put me away, and the FBI wants me to walk the tight rope between the two.

I don't have a good plan yet, but whatever I end up doing I will need money. This two hundred grand will go a long way to getting me set up somewhere warm, sunny, and with plenty of sandy beaches.

"I'm here, aren't I?" Hawk asks,

running his fingers over his bald head as if there was hair there.

"I don't wait," I say. "Another ten minutes and I wouldn't have been here anymore."

Something between a scoff and a snort escapes his lips. "So, you do wait but only for twenty minutes, is that right?" he asks.

Hawk's cocky and arrogant and I don't mean that as a compliment. He is the type to make you wait because he thinks your time is less valuable than his.

It's not. He is on his way to becoming an associate in a crime syndicate.

He wears the gold chain and the expensive suit because he wants to be noticed. Acknowledged. Seen.

I commit crimes so that I can be invisible. I want to be a ghost. The problem is that, now that I'm back home, I haven't been particularly successful at it.

"If you are not going to act professional," I say slowly and quietly to show him that I am not intimidated. "I will not do anymore jobs for you or your boss. And when he asks me why I'm suddenly working for his competitors I'll explain that it's because of you."

His eyes narrow out of anger. He purses his lips and then takes a deep breath. "It won't happen again," he finally concedes.

It's not exactly an apology but he's the type who thinks that to apologize is to show weakness, when in reality it's to show strength. But his statement is enough for now.

"Do you have it?" he asks. I give him a nod. "Where is it?"

"It's nearby," I say without blinking. "Where is the money?"

"Nearby as well."

I take a sip of my coffee and pour some maple syrup on my stack of pancakes.

I have played this game before.

I am pretty sure that he has, too.

"So?" Hawk is the first one to break our silence.

When the waitress came by with the

menu and a pot of coffee, he said no to both.

That's his prerogative but the food in this hole-in-the-wall diner is to die for.

"So what?" I ask, biting into the fluffiest pancake I've ever had. It tastes like I'm eating a sugary cloud.

"How are we going to do this... exchange?" he asks.

He taps his fingers on the vinyl seat. I hear him crack his knuckles and wipe his palms on his pants.

"You are going to slide that bag you have in your lap over to me. When I am certain that everything is there then I'll hand you the flash drive," I say and take another forkful of the pancake.

At a loss as to what to do, he acquiesces and does as he is told.

He hands me the bag under the table and I count the stacks of one hundred dollar bills.

When I am satisfied that there is two hundred grand in there, I leave a twenty on the table and get up from the table.

"Hey, aren't you forgetting something," Hawk says, his eyes widening out of fear. I extend my hand for him to shake.

"It has been a pleasure doing business with you," I say, pressing the flash drive into his palm. The lines around his eyes relax and he smiles. "You reach out if you have anymore work for me in the future."

## 28

## NICHOLAS
### WHEN WE LOOK FOR HIM...

My phone goes off as soon as I get into the car.

It's Olive. Her voice sounds frantic.

As soon as she calls, I see the string of text messages that she had sent me while I was talking to Hawk.

"What's wrong?" I ask.

"He's gone. I can't find him anywhere. He won't return my calls. They took him," she says.

She talks fast, running over the last sentence with the next.

I takes me a moment to realize that she's talking about Owen.

"He's probably fine, Olive," I say to

comfort her. "He probably just went to see a girl."

"No, he hasn't," she insists. "He wouldn't do that without telling me. Or texting me."

I think about it for a moment.

I don't know much about Owen so she may be right.

But then something occurs to me.

"Does he even know how to text?" I ask.

"I showed him how to use the phone."

"I know but it's not exactly the same thing as having one and using one all the time. What if he forgot it somewhere? What if he doesn't expect that he needs to check in with you like a ten year old."

I regret the last sentence even before the words escape my lips.

"If you don't want to help then you don't have to but I thought you would at least try to be a little more compassionate," she snaps back and hangs up.

I call her back immediately and luckily, she does pick up.

"Where are you?" I ask.

I pick her up a few minutes later. When I pull up to the curb, I see her pacing back and forth with her arms crossed at her chest, holding on to herself.

She has a faraway look in her eyes and there are lines on her forehead that I have not seen before, worry lines.

Climbing into the car, she lets out a big sigh of relief as if now she is not going to be the only one carrying the burden.

"I don't know where he is. He didn't come home last night," she starts to rattle off as soon as she clicks her seat belt buckle in. "I thought that maybe he went to see that woman he met in prison but she's not replying to my calls either. He didn't come home this morning and then he didn't call all day. It's just not really like him. I mean, I know that he's a grown up but he's living with me and he just got out of prison and he doesn't have any money."

She lets out a big sigh, probably

realizing that she has not taken a breath since she started on her rant.

I am not entirely sure what to do. If Owen is just out having a good time, the last thing he wants is to have us crashing that for him.

Or maybe he's doing this because he's mad at her. Perhaps he's angry with her for spending time with me. Maybe he just wants to make her pay for going against him.

If it were up to me, I'd do nothing.

A guy who has spent that much time in prison is due for some rest and relaxation and that typically doesn't involve spending twelve hours a day cooped up with his sister.

"You don't think it's a big deal, do you?" Olive asks.

I shrug a little. She turns to me and shakes her head. Her eyes have a look in them filled with disappointment, it's as if I had just run over her new puppy.

"Okay, let's go," I finally say.

"Where?"

"We are going to find Owen."

Her face immediately lights up. This is what she had wanted the whole time.

She'd come to see me for a shrug, or for me to tell her that he is probably fine. She came to me for an answer, whatever it may be.

So, I'll give her one. Or at least, do my best to find her one.

We drive back to her apartment, the last place where Owen was seen. I am not entirely sure if the fact that his stuff is still there is a good sign or not but I ask her to help me go through it to find out anything that we can about who he might have gone to see. The first person on my list is the teacher.

"Do you know her name?" I ask, walking over to his stacks of stuff in the living room by the couch.

They were once packed neatly into two duffel bags but are now scattered in piles underneath the windowsill.

"I don't think we should be touching his stuff," Olive says.

"It's the only thing we have to go on."

She nods and sits down next to me to look through his papers.

"She came to work there a year or two ago, but he never told me her name. I think she also lives in Boston."

"So, she drove all the way out to the prison for that job?" I ask.

She shrugs. "She worked in a few community colleges so her commute between classes was pretty bad. But her schedule changed every semester. I don't know exactly how long she worked at the prison."

Leafing through the fifth notebook of his poems and diary entries, trying to find some relevant information without too much invasion of privacy, I see a name scribbled sideways at the end of the last one.

There's a number and email address written underneath. The email is an official one issued from Roxbury Community College.

I grab my phone and look it up. She's listed on the bottom of the English department roster of teachers: *Gabrielle Aston Moore, adjunct*

"That's her. That's Gabby," she says, pointing to the name in the back of his notebook.

## 29

## NICHOLAS
### WHEN WE FIND HER...

I t doesn't take long to find her home address and discover that she lives about twenty minutes away.

At first, Olive wants to call her and to ask but I insist that we go there and, if at all possible, see for ourselves if Owen is there.

"He may just be hiding out there and making you worry on purpose," I explain. She isn't too sure about this but agrees anyway.

When we get to Gabby's door, Olive can't bring herself to knock so I step in. A woman in pajamas holding a slice of pizza answers the door. Her hair, cropped short to the ear, keeps falling in her face.

"I got it!" she yells back into the living room. "Can I help you?"

The rain turns from a drizzle to pouring down sheets and we inch closer to her on her non-existent porch to get under the awning.

I wait for Olive to start talking but she doesn't.

"This is Olive Kernes, her brother is Owen Kernes. We believe you taught him in prison," I say.

Before I can ask her about his whereabouts, she shuts the front door behind her and steps out into the rain.

"What do you want?" she asks, glancing back to make sure that noone inside hears us.

"My brother is missing. I haven't seen him for almost twenty-four hours," Olive says. "I know that you two were...are in a relationship."

"We are not!" she snaps.

Her pants flap in the wind and she

pulls her pajamas tightly around her body as she crosses her arms.

"I'm sorry, I'm not here to make any accusations...I just don't know where he is. I thought that he might be here with you."

"Well, he's not. I haven't seen him since he was inside."

I can't tell if she's lying about that or is just very nervous about whoever is inside finding out what she is talking about here.

"Gabby, you can trust us. We won't tell anyone about your relationship," I say. "We just want to find Owen."

"Our relationship? Are you crazy?" she says, pursing her lips. "I was his teacher and he was my student. Nothing else."

I try to read her but she's a closed book.

"I'd like you to leave now," she says, opening the door to sneak back inside.

"Hey, Gabby!" a man says, walking past the foyer. "What are you doing? Are you okay?"

He is right in front of us before she can stop him. "Why are you talking out there? Oh my god, you're soaked!"

The man is about her age, in his thirties, also dressed in sweats.

"They were just leaving," Gabby says, with her eyes pleading with mine to go away.

"Hi, I'm Mike, Gabby's husband." The man extends his hand to me.

He has the friendly and outgoing demeanor of a middle school gym teacher, the exact opposite of his wife.

As my mind races to decide whether we should go with our real names or another identity, Olive shakes his hand and introduces herself.

"Your wife taught my brother when she worked in the prison system. He always had the best things to say about her...as a teacher. She was a real inspiration."

"Oh, wow, is that so, honey? That's wonderful."

"Anyway, he got out on parole just a bit ago and he has been staying with me...

and now, unfortunately, I haven't heard from him since last night. It's really not like him to just take off. I'm worried that something terrible has happened. I found Ms. Moore's, Gabby's, email address in the back of his notebooks and I thought I would come by and see if you had heard from him."

Gabby clenches her jaw and forces a compassionate nod when she really wants to tear Olive's throat out. "Like I said, I haven't heard from him for a while now."

Back in the car, Olive asks me if I believe her. I think about it for a moment. Gabby was definitely not happy to see us.

She wanted nothing more than to make us go away and that makes me think that if she had known where Owen was then she would have told us.

I don't know where Olive stands on this because she just buries her head in her hands and begins to cry.

"Okay, it seems like she was telling us the truth." I finally reach a decision. Olive is distraught. She doesn't know what to do (or think) and someone has to. "Now, let's try to think of where else he could be or who would know where he could have gone."

"His parole officer?" Olive asks. I shake my head no.

"He's the last person who should know anything about this."

"Why?" she asks in a meek tone.

"I don't want to get him in trouble. If he's doing something illegal or hanging out with someone he shouldn't be, we can't let the parole officer know that. He'll just send him back to prison."

Olive begins to shake, beginning at her shoulders and quickly spreading throughout her body.

I've never seen her this worried. I know that it has been over twenty-four hours but he's a grown man. He's not a child. Adults are free to come and go as they please, especially ones that have been cooped up in a tiny room for most of their lives. She has to know this, right?

And it hits me.

"Is there something you're not telling

me?" I ask, turning to face her. She shakes her head no, but then bites her lower lip and looks away.

"What is it?" I ask. "I can't help if I don't know everything, Olive. What's going on?"

Looking out of the passenger seat's window, she stares at the massive trunk of an old tree whose roots have split the cement slabs in quarters, raising them into the air.

"They said that they would only do it if you hadn't given them the hard drive," she finally says with a whimper. "It hasn't been that long. Why would they do it so...quickly?"

My blood runs cold. The tips of my hands go numb. What is she talking about?

"You gave them the flash drive, right?" she asks, snapping her body back into its seat to face me. I furrow my brow and open my mouth to speak. But nothing comes out.

"I gave it to my client, yes," I confirm.

She lets out a sigh of relief, but that only makes my chest tighten further.

She shouldn't know anything about him and what does this have to do with Owen?

"So, why is he gone then?" she asks.

"Hawk has nothing to do with Owen," I say, catching myself saying his name when it is already too late.

"Hawk?" Olive looks up at me, shaking her head. "No, Janet Bailey. Wasn't that who you were supposed to give the flash drive to?"

Now, it's my turn to sink back in my seat and give her a blank stare. "I have no idea who that is," I say under my breath. "Who is she?"

"No, you have to know her," Olive insists. "That's probably not her real name. But she works for the same person you and your partner were working for when you did the Martha's Vineyard job."

Beads of cold sweat run down my sides. How does she know anything about that? And why?

"Janet came to see me," Olive

explains, reading my mind. "She said that her boss was upset by you taking off like that and that you owe him a debt. But if I help you get that flash drive then it'll go a long way to paying it off."

My ears start to buzz and I can barely hear a word coming out of her mouth. I focus on her lips to try to understand what she is saying.

"She said I had to help you because if you didn't get the drive, then they'd do something to Owen. She told me there's a bounty on his head. You were right. He flipped on some bad guys in prison and gave evidence to the state. That's why he got out early. But if you got that flash drive then they wouldn't hurt him."

I try to focus but my vision is blurry. It takes ten minutes for each second to pass as I lose myself in a trance, with my body here but my mind somewhere far away.

"Are you listening to me, Nicholas?" Olive grabs my thigh.

I focus my eyes on her grip, her left hand on my right thigh, and finally it comes into focus.

She doesn't wait for me to respond before continuing to talk. "I don't know why they would've hurt him so early. I mean, you just delivered the flash drive. No, it can't be them. Something else must have happened. Maybe you're right, maybe he's just getting drunk with some of his old buddies and I'm worried about everything for no reason."

## 30

## OLIVE
WHEN THE PUZZLE PIECES DON'T FIT...

T alking to Nicholas always makes me feel better. He isn't the type to cut in and suggest solutions.

Sometimes when you are having a shitty day, the last thing you want is a to-do list of how you should fix it.

No, Nicholas isn't like that.

He gives me exactly what I don't know I need.

He listens. He nods and holds me and tells me that everything is going to be okay.

As we talk in the parked car outside of Gabby's house, I am still not sure whether she's telling us the truth. She was a little too eager to get us away, but then again, she's married.

I don't know if Owen knew that or not or perhaps he just didn't care. The person that didn't know for sure was her friendly and helpful husband and she wanted to do everything in her power to keep it that way.

So, what does that mean exactly? Would it make her lie about Owen's whereabouts?

The more I think about it, the less sure I am.

If she actually knew where he was then it would've taken her a lot less time to convey that than to convince us that she hadn't seen him in months.

Then again, the truth can be somewhere in between. She has seen him.

She doesn't want to tell us this because she's hiding her affair from her husband.

She doesn't want to talk about her infidelity to complete strangers because that's two more people who know about the secret. That's two more people who can tell her husband the truth.

I convey most of these thoughts in a long-winded stream of consciousness that pretty much goes in circles.

Nicholas listens carefully, nods occasionally but is generally absent, lost in his own thoughts. He stares at my hand on his thigh for a long time before finally meeting my eyes.

He takes a deep breath before saying, "I didn't give the flash drive to Janet Bailey," he says, choosing each word with caution.

My forehead tenses as I lean closer to him to make sure that I heard him right.

"I don't know who she is but Hawk does not work for my old boss," he adds.

"Who's Hawk?" I whisper, suddenly very well aware of how dry my mouth is.

"A client," he says. "He paid me two hundred grand to do this job and that's what I did."

One of his eyelashes is curled under the others. He rubs his eye but it doesn't straighten out.

"Olive, did you hear me?"

When he touches his palm to the back of my hand, a jolt of electricity rushes through me and pulls me out of this trance.

"No, no, no," I say. "They must work for the same person. You just don't know."

This reminds me of being ten years old and putting together one of those thousand-piece puzzles that I got at the thrift store. Unlike the other ones, there are no pieces missing and I get excited that I'm finally going to finish this one all the way to the end.

And then something else happens. The pieces don't fit.

I rotate them and try them any which way but they still don't snap into place.

It's only after I look a little closer do I realize that this piece belongs to the New York skyline not San Francisco's.

"Olive, this job has nothing to do with repaying any debt for that Harry Winston necklace. I didn't have a debt. Our so-called boss was talking to the FBI and recording all of his jobs to turn us in. He's gone now. In the witness protection program with a new identity, living in some suburb of Tucson or Portland or Orlando. I have no idea where he is but he's out of commission now."

I listen and nod but nothing registers. At least, not the way it's supposed to. I was so certain that the flash drive was meant for the same client that it never even occurred to me to ask. And now, what's going to happen now?

My nose starts to tingle and thick heavy tears roll down my face. They burn my eyes and I can't wipe them off quickly enough before the next round comes down. Nicholas wraps his arms around me.

"What does this mean? What's happened?" I mumble through the sobs.

"Whoever came to see you, this Janet Bailey, she wants the flash drive but we don't have it anymore," Nicholas says.

I want him to sugarcoat it. I want him to outright lie. But he doesn't and that makes things even worse.

"So, they took him? That's why he's missing, right," I say, shaking my head with my whole body shaking.

"Not necessarily," Nicholas says. A glimmer of hope, perhaps?

"What do you mean?"

"I'm not sure what happened to him. One, he could just be out somewhere. He's not used to carrying that phone around or answering it or maybe he just forgot it somewhere," Nicholas suggests.

I wipe my face and then wipe my hands on my pants. I wait to hear more.

"Two, something could've happened to him but it may not be related to the flash drive. You said that Janet said that people want to kill him?"

I nod. "Apparently, his boss put out a bounty. Anyone who kills him and proves it will get one hundred thousand dollars."

Nicholas picks at the seam along the steering wheel with this index finger.

"That's a pretty big bounty," he says after a moment. "I don't want to lie to you, Olive, but whatever he did, whomever he turned in, they are really fucking mad."

I press my nails into the soft part of my palm until I feel pain.

"As far as bad news goes, if something did happen to him it may or may not be related to the flash drive. I'm not entirely sure if Janet Bailey and her people are responsible since it did happen so... quickly. They have waited a long time to get paid back, why not wait a little more to get the flash drive?"

My tears have dried and my thoughts are more focused but none of that gives me the answer that I want. Then something hits me. "What's even on that flash drive?" I ask.

## 31

## NICHOLAS
### WHEN WE MEET UP...

I don't know what's on the flash drive and I make it a point to not know these things. I am just the quintessential middleman. I'm a courier. I'm a post office worker.

It's not my job to know what's in the parcels that I deliver, in fact it would be harder for me to do my job if I did know. When I tell Olive this, she doesn't seem to believe me. I try to convince her but I'm not particularly effective.

The thing is that I can't know what's in the package, not if I want to get more jobs. If I were to find out that something I'm taking and delivering is worth say one million dollars and they are only paying me two hundred grand then I would be tempted to cut them out of the deal. Of course, it's worth much more than what they're paying me to get it.

Otherwise they wouldn't make a profit on it and everyone in this business has to get paid.

We don't do this for fun (well, not the sane ones, anyway). We do it for money.

But the job is not without its perks. There are no set schedules and there is no office. There is a boss or at least a client that you want to please in order to get more work in the future.

Not long ago, I thought that the Harry Winston necklace would be it for me. That would be my ticket out but it didn't turn out that way.

That's why I'm back here, trying to build up my savings.

If I want to keep Olive happy and pay her the money that I promised then I'll need to do more jobs like his one over the next year.

Finding Owen isn't really in the plans,

but Olive needs an answer and there is someone who might have one.

*Why am I not there with you?* She texts and my phone dings.

I put it on vibrate.

We have already had this conversation. I am meeting with a contact who might know something. I told her about him when I felt sorry for her but now standing in the alley, watching my breath rise above me in a puff, I regret every part of that spill.

She can't be here because she can't know that I'm talking to the FBI. She thinks I'm meeting with an old acquaintance who knows the run of the streets. What she doesn't know, what no one will ever know, is that I'm in a lot of trouble with the federal government.

They have a whole file on me and they are using it to get information. When my well runs dry or I stop cooperating and doing independent research for them (basically when I stop doing their job for them), they are going to throw the book at me.

The details of that particular book, I am not so sure of though. Is it just the prior crimes that will come before a jury? Or will they also charge me with all of the shitty things I did, to get the precious information that they want.

"What do you have for me?" Art Hedison asks, walking toward me. He is dressed in a nice suit and shoes, clearly doing something outside of his capacity as an FBI agent.

"Where are you going? Coming from?" I ask, trying to be friendly. This hasn't always been my approach but I figured I'd give it a try this time since I do need him to do me a favor.

"My sister's engagement party. Why are we meeting? What's so important?"

He doesn't have time for this. That could be a good thing. Maybe I can get a quick answer and a goodbye.

"Owen Kernes is...missing."

Art stares at me and then lets out a big hollow laugh originating somewhere in the pit of his stomach.

"You don't believe me?" I ask. "So, you know where he is?"

His laughter subsides quickly and the corners of his mouth start to point downward.

"What the fuck is going on, Crawford?" he asks. At least, he didn't call me Nicky again. "You were supposed to befriend him and get him to talk to you. What the fuck have you been doing instead?"

"That's what I have been trying to do," I insist. "I was friendly. I was nice but it's kind of hard to get a guy to like you if he thinks you're the one who murdered his girlfriend."

Art shuffles his feet, popping a cigarette into his mouth.

"But this isn't about that. Olive told me that she hasn't seen him since Saturday. She doesn't know where he is and she's worried. I'm sure that you are aware of that bounty that they have on his head."

"Who?" Art asks, revealing nothing.

"I don't know who. I just know that

there is one. One hundred grand, to be paid to anyone who kills him and shows proof. Someone is really mad at whatever he did inside to get out."

It takes Art a few moments to process all of this information. I lean back against the wall as he thinks it over.

"So, what you're telling me is that he's dead? And that you don't have a job to do anymore?" he asks, taking a drag of his cigarette and blowing it in my face.

"No, what I'm telling you is that I've been helping Olive track him down but there's only so much we can do. I was hoping that you could help us. Maybe talk to the cops? Find out something?"

"Listen to me, you asshole." Art puts his finger in my face. "I'm not here to do you any favors or to make your life easier. That's what you do for me. So, go do that. Find out where he is and get on his good side. Otherwise, you're going to get on my bad one."

I resist the temptation to roll my eyes and I wonder why I thought this was such a good idea. Then I remember.

I had to see his face when I told him that Owen is missing.

Art doesn't have a good poker face and I now know for sure that he has no idea where Owen is.

## 32

## OLIVE

### WHEN I THINK OF ANOTHER POSSIBILITY...

Nicholas doesn't ask me about her and seeing her again is the last thing I want to do, but I have to make sure that he's not there. When we get back to my apartment, I pour each of us a generous amount of whiskey and down mine immediately.

The thought of doing this makes me want to drink the whole bottle but then I won't remember anything and that's never a positive thing in an investigation. Nicholas nurses his drink, watching me get another helping.

"You planning on blacking out tonight?" he asks.

I raise my eyebrows in disapproval and he quickly throws up his hands to admit defeat.

"I'm not saying you can't, I'm just... interested in what our plans are," he adds.

"I don't have any plans," I lie. "I just want to have some drinks and not think about him anymore."

We sit in silence for a bit, listening to the apartment settling into itself. This place is newer, so nothing creaks here like it used to in all of those places growing up.

It's no wonder there are about a million different movies and books set in New England and about ninety percent of them involve ghosts. I don't have any supernatural beings haunting me, but that doesn't mean that I'm not haunted.

"There is one more person we should probably go see if we want to make sure to dot all of our i's and cross all of our t's," I say, throwing back the last of my second drink.

Nicholas leans back against the couch

and puts his foot on top of his bended knee.

"And who's that?" he asks when I don't go further.

"My mother," I say after a long pause.

"When do you want to go?" he asks, without taking a beat.

I shake my head. "No, not tonight. It's late and I've had the shittiest day in a long time."

I pick at the flower on the shawl that's draped over the couch. It's the color of a sunset and it always gave me a good feeling looking at it, especially on all of those short dark and gloomy winter days.

Tonight, however, it doesn't do its job.

"You think he went to see his mother?" Nicholas asks.

"Yes... No... I don't know. Maybe. He shouldn't have. I told him what she did to me. But you know how people are with their mothers."

Nicholas exhales slowly, his nostrils flaring.

"I know how some people are," he finally says.

We haven't talked about his relationship with his mother much, but right now is not a good time.

I pour myself another glass, this time of wine, and offer one to him as well. He sticks to whiskey.

Half an hour later he is quite buzzed and I'm outright drunk.

"You know, I wanted to have some drinks with you because I thought it would cheer me up," I admit.

"Has it?"

I shake my head no. "Now, I just want to cry."

I lean my head into his shoulder and he pulls up my chin toward his face.

"Alcohol always makes you cry, even if it makes you laugh first," he says, placing his lips softly on mine.

I tilt my head further back and open my mouth. Our tongues touch and a little burst of electricity rushes through me.

He pulls down my shirt, exposing my breasts. He takes one into his mouth, taking the other one in his hand. His tongue feels soft and firm on my nipple and I arch my body with each kiss.

He takes turns between the two to make sure that neither is neglected and a warm soothing sensation starts to build at my core.

After freeing me of my top and bra, he starts to run his tongue and mouth down my body. He starts at the top near the nape of my neck and slowly makes his way down to my belly button and to my pelvic bones.

Then he pulls the top of my panties slightly down and out of the way, teasing me.

I bury my hands in his hair. Its soft, thick strands slide around my fingers making them difficult to grip.

His fingers touch the inside of my thighs and my legs immediately open wide.

Every part of me is so aroused that I feel flushed and damp at the same time. My breasts feel heavy and sensitive along with other parts of my skin.

His fingers make their way inside of

me, teasing me, playing with me. When he reaches over to kiss me, I slide mine down his body, shocked to find that he has already stripped himself of all clothing.

I wrap my hand around his hard, big cock and listen to him moan into my ear.

We lose ourselves in our hands and in the energy that they create, occasionally pressing our lips to each other's in a sloping sideways kiss.

Slowly, I turn on my side, raising my leg a little in the air and keeping my hand firmly around him. For a moment, he pulls away and I hear a snap of latex somewhere behind me before he glides inside.

As his movements speed up, the urgency and the heat that he has generated in between my legs pushes me over the edge. I call out his name as I try to catch my breath while waves of pleasure course through my body.

## 33

## OLIVE

### WHEN WE GO TO SEE HER...

The stoop of my mother's building is lined with rotten wood. I trip on one of these panels and nearly fall on my face, catching myself with my hands and getting a large gash across my palm.

Perfect, I think to myself. What a perfect way to start the day.

It's a little bit after noon and I hope it's a good time to catch her. She's not much of a morning person and she often goes on a bender late at night, sleeping in until eleven is not uncommon.

What I hope is that she didn't start on her new day's drinking yet.

The hallway smells as if someone

urinated in it recently because someone probably has, and it takes three loud, police department are here to arrest someone, type of knocks, to get her to open the door.

"What the fuck are you doing here?" my mother asks.

Standing before her in her tattered robe, unwashed hair, and dark circles underneath her eyes, I can't help but wonder the same thing.

"I'm looking for Owen," I say, crossing my arms. "Have you seen him?"

"Hi, who's your friend here?" she asks, extending her hand.

Given how friendly she's being, I'm thinking she's already had a drink or four. They shake hands and she smiles when he calls her Mrs. Kernes.

"You can just call her..." I start to say.

"Mrs. Kernes is fine," she cuts me off. "It's about time I got some respect around here. Would you like to come in, Mr. Crawford?"

Nicholas flashes me a smile as a sign for thumbs up and follows her inside.

"Olive, you coming?" she hollers back at me and I reluctantly come inside.

The apartment smells like stale cigarettes and is covered in dust and garbage. She has never been one for picking up after herself, but I don't remember it ever being this bad.

I would always clean up whenever I came by, whether it was to do dishes or sweep the floor.

But now, the dirt and debris are just piling up along with the boxes of deliveries, dirty clothes, and grocery bags.

My mother doesn't seem at all bothered by any of this. There are people out there who apologize for the mess in a clean apartment, but my mother doesn't even offer one for this.

Then again, we did just turn up at her door unannounced without even a phone call.

"So... how's Owen?" she asks. "I heard he got out."

"You haven't seen him?"

"Nope. I would've appreciated it if he had stopped by. I mean, what has it been?

Ten years since we saw each other on the outside?" She lights a cigarette and blows the smoke high into the air.

"Did you visit him in prison?" Nicholas asks.

"A few times, but it's hard for me to get around, you know. I'm sure that Olive told you."

"The reason we're here, Mom, is...he hasn't come back home for two nights. And I'm worried about him."

It's hard for me to put myself out like this with my mother. I wish I had the kind of relationship with her where I could talk to her about anything but we don't.

Even before she did what she did, I always kept my cards close to my chest. She never made me feel safe enough to reveal who I really was or what I was going through.

"How's he doing?" my mom asks, melting into the recliner in front of the television.

She doesn't invite us to sit down and I

want to leave. I try to get Nicholas'
attention but he doesn't acknowledge me.

"He's fine. Was fine when he was
staying with me. But now...I'm not so
sure."

"Eh, you know men. He probably
needed to get out there and get some. He
hasn't been with a girl in a decade."

"Okay, let's go Nicholas," I say, turning
around on my heels.

"Leaving so soon?" she yells after me.

"Yep. If you haven't seen him then I
have nothing else to say to you."

I open the front door and wave
Nicholas over.

"Oh, c'mon, don't be like that, Olive.
Why can't we start again? Oh, are *you* that
dashing mysterious man who wrote her
the letter and got her to go to Hawaii?"
she asks Nicholas.

I don't hear his answer.

I'm too dumbstruck by the person
standing before me at the bottom of the
stairs.

"Owen?" I whisper. My voice is barely

audible. Something tickles my throat and I cough.

A sudden gush of rain starts to beat down on us. It was only a drizzle before, but now it's strong enough to make the shrubs next to the railing quiver under the weight of each drop.

Owen rushes past me without saying a word, up the stairs to our mother's door. But I can't move. It's as if my feet have been shackled to the ground by some invisible force.

"C'mon, it's pouring!" he yells from the doorstep.

"Where have you been?" I scream to hear myself over the storm.

He doesn't reply and just disappears behind the door. I follow him inside.

As soon as I see him put her bag of takeout on the table, I know that my mother was lying. Of course, I think to myself.

Why wouldn't she? She has always been a deceitful asshole, why did I think that had changed?

I'm tempted to just turn around and leave but I also want answers.

"I've been looking for you," I say with water dripping off me onto the welcome mat. "Why didn't you call me? Why didn't you tell me you were here?"

He turns toward our mom and says, "Mother, you care to explain?"

Mom smiles in her cunning way and shrugs her shoulders in an exaggerated way.

"I'm sorry, okay?" she says to Owen. "You see, what happened was that I borrowed his phone when he went to get a pack of cigarettes and I broke it."

I roll my eyes.

"Here, if you don't believe me." Owen hands it to me.

If it had been dropped, the screen would be cracked. But this phone was shattered.

It wouldn't even turn on. It looked like it had been thrown against the wall or hit with something really heavy. Whatever happened to it, happened to it on purpose.

"I didn't know your number," Owen says, opening the containers of Indian food and placing them on the counter.

Something is different about him. He's here, but he's not here. It's like he's absent.

"She has my number," I point out.

"Yeah, but you said you never wanted to hear from me again," my mother points out, gesturing with her cigarette.

That doesn't mean that you couldn't have given it to him, I want to say but instead, I focus my attention on Owen.

"You could have just come back and told me."

He shrugs and gives me a vapid smile. His eyes won't meet mine and it's not just because of the guilt. There is something else going on.

## 34

## OLIVE

### WHEN WE GO OUT ON THE STOOP...

Owen doesn't say anything for some time. I watch him arrange all of the containers in a buffet-style. Once he's done, he walks over to me and throws his arm around my shoulder.

"Olive, I'm sorry," he says, somewhat slurring his words. "Honestly, I know you didn't want me to go see Mom but I had to. She's my mother, you know. I missed her. I haven't seen her in a long time."

"I wouldn't have said anything about that. But I was worried. You should've told me."

"Eh, you weren't that worried," he says, waving his hand in my face.

His words are slow but not deliberate. He seems oddly relaxed given that he is in Nicholas' presence. "Besides, you have him. You made your choice."

I pull away from him.

"What are you talking about? Made my choice? Nicholas is my boyfriend and you're my brother. I have room in my life for both of you."

"Nah, nope, nada," Owen says. "That's where you're wrong. You don't have room for both of us. He killed my girlfriend and I can't be around someone like that. And you...you made it real clear the last time we talked that you believe him."

"I never said anything like that. But you're making accusations about him that you can't know for sure are true."

"I know, Olive!" Owen raises his voice. "I know what he did and what he didn't do! And if you believe him over me, then *fuck* you!"

"Is that why you're here? Is that why you made me look for you all over town? I was this close," I say, pushing my thumb and index finger together, leaving only a sliver of space between the two, "I was this close to going to your parole officer."

"You were going to do what?" Owen yells. It originates somewhere deep in his stomach and comes out like a roar. "Don't you *ever* talk to him! This is a personal matter, Olive. This is none of your business."

"There are people trying to kill you, you asshole! Whoever you snitched on in prison, they are connected big time and there's a ticking clock on your life. So when you didn't show up, and I didn't see you for two days, I thought you were dead."

Sobs that had started to gather in the back of my throat have turned into tears that stream down my face when I say the last bit. They are a mixture of anger and disappointment and disillusionment.

"I know that, don't you think I know that?" he asks.

"No, I don't. Otherwise, I don't think you would be here, getting high with Mom and making me look for you all over town."

Owen takes a drag of his cigarette and leans over the counter for support. He doesn't say anything for a few moments and the silence in the room becomes overbearing.

"The food is getting cold," Mom says. "Would you like to have some, Nicholas?"

"No, thank you," he mumbles.

"Suit yourself," she says, piling food from different containers onto a plastic plate.

"Can we talk somewhere...in private?" Owen asks.

I nod and follow him out onto the stoop. The rain is still pouring down and we huddle under the small, ripped awning.

"What the fuck are you doing here?" I say in a hushed tone.

It's the middle of the day but I don't want the neighbors to hear what they have already heard plenty of.

"I wanted to see her. I knew that you wouldn't approve and I didn't want to have a fight about it," he says coldly.

"I was worried about you. I wish you had called."

Looking somewhere behind me, he says, "I was going to, but she broke my phone. On purpose. She said she wanted some alone time with me. That she missed me. Then we got high and... honestly, Olive, it was like a day later and I completely lost track of time."

"Yeah, meth will do that to you," I say, my words heavy with judgement.

He lets the words roll off his back and doesn't call me on it. I'm his concerned sister who doesn't want him to do hard drugs (or any drugs for that matter) but I shouldn't have said that. That self-centered and better-than-thou bullshit isn't going to do anyone any good.

"I know that I'm not supposed to use anymore. You know that I had a problem when I was a kid, before I went to prison. And then everything just got worse in there."

"You can get drugs in prison?" I ask, naively.

"You can get anything in there. And

drugs are one of the easiest, a lot easier than a cell phone, for instance. Being high helps you pass the time like nothing else," Owen says, looking far away at the horizon, as if he can see behind all of those dilapidated buildings. "Then, when I learned to read, I quit."

"So, what happened?" I ask. "Why did you...do this?"

"I wanted to see Mom," he says quietly. "I didn't want to have a fight with you about it. We have been fighting about enough. But seeing her brought back all of this anger and guilt and everything else that I felt for so long. She was always so selfish and she never looked out for us."

"So, why didn't you call me? Why didn't you come back to me once you saw that?"

"I don't know." He shrugs. "I know that she was a shitty mother but she is my mother and she's the only one I'll ever have. So, I just wanted for things to be good between us again. I didn't want to feel so crappy about everything. I didn't want to think about all of terrible things that she did when I was a kid. I just wanted to be happy with her. So, when she offered me a beer, I said yes. When she offered me a joint, I said yes. And then...she offered me some meth and, again, I said yes."

He hangs his head so far down that his chin almost touches his chest.

I can't help but feel sorry for him and my hand reaches for his. As soon as we touch, he pulls me in closer and buries his face in my shoulder.

I hold him through the hard thick sobs of regret and promise him that everything will be alright.

I'm no longer angry with him. I am here for him and I want to make his pain go away.

"I have to tell you something," I say when we pull away from one another. "We went to see Gabby."

It takes him a moment to process this information before asking why in a flat effect.

"We were looking for you and we

found her email address in your notebook and looked her up."

"You shouldn't have done that," Owen says. "She's married."

"Yes, I found that out when her husband came out."

"Does he know about me?" he asks after a moment.

"No, I just said I was your sister and she taught you in class, that was it. But she wasn't very happy to see me. Have you talked to her recently?"

"Not since I got out."

I don't know if that's a good thing or not as I give him a reassuring nod.

"The thing is that...there's somebody else. Someone I can't have, and no one can really ever compare to her."

I look at him surprised.

My heart skips a beat, in a good way though.

People meet people in prison all the time but this sounds like it's something serious. Why hadn't he said anything about this before?

"This is great, Owen," I say, giving him a hug. "Who is she? Tell me everything."

"No, it's not," he says quietly. "It's not important. I can't have her. She's...off limits."

"Like married?" I ask.

I don't like this streak of him dating married women. He's better than that or at least he should be.

"Does she have a family?" I ask with a wince.

The thought of my brother breaking up a family with kids makes me nauseated. I know what it is to be on the other end of that. I suspect that's one of the reasons why our father disappeared so much for days or weeks at a time when I was a kid.

It's not like Mom was a particularly easy person to live with but she didn't deserve to be yanked around like that.

He cheated on her, they fought, he left and then he came back and the cycle started all over again.

"No, she doesn't," he says to my relief.

"So, she has a husband but no kids?" I double check.

"No, she's not married," he says quietly.

"Okay...so, what's the problem then? If she has a boyfriend or a fiancé, it's great but she's not married yet," I say, gasping to myself silently for what I just said.

It's not okay if she's married and it's not okay if she's with someone. It's lying and deceiving and shitty all around.

"No, she doesn't have a boyfriend, not really," Owen says.

I narrow my eyes and try to figure out the problem. When he doesn't elaborate I grab him by the shoulders and shake him a little.

"So...go get her. Why haven't you yet? Why are you being so secretive about this?"

The first gunshot sounds like thunder. The second sounds like a firecracker.

Blood rushes to my head. There's nowhere to hide. I drop down to the stairs but on top of the stoop, I'm completely exposed.

Someone yells in the distance. I focus my eyes and see a group of guys in a gray Cadillac with the windows rolled down.

The guy in the passenger seat is a holding a big gun with a long barrel. Another shot goes off.

This one hits right above my head, at least it feels like it does.

I cover my face with my hands and don't look up until the car screeches away.

That's when I see Owen with his blood all over the top step.

"Owen! Owen!" I slide over to him, cradling his head in my lap. "Everything is going to be okay. I'm here."

I wipe his face with my hands and kiss him on his eyes and cheeks over and over again.

"Someone, please call the police! He needs the paramedics!" I yell at the top of my lungs.

His eyes are open and he blinks with every other breath or so.

Blood is literally draining away his

face, turning his pale skin even more white.

"Olive," he says slowly and with great difficulty.

"You're going to be fine," I repeat myself in a frantic tone trying to make both of us believe what might be completely impossible.

"Olive," he says again, raising his finger slightly as if to get me to be quiet.

Wiping tears off my cheek, I let out a big sob and wait.

"I...love...you," he says with a long pause between each word.

"I love you, too. So much." I grab and hug him as hard as I can wanting nothing more than to somehow infuse him with life.

The paramedics arrive and the world gets the volume turned down. I watch everything as if it's happening to someone else.

When I look up, I realize that Nicholas is right behind me.

I don't know how long he has been

there and I turn my body toward his chest and fall into his open arms.

"He's going to be okay. They are taking him to the hospital. He's going to pull through," he whispers into my ear.

## 35

## OLIVE
### WHILE I WAIT...

The hospital smells like cleaning products. The waiting room is brightly lit and a place in which it's impossible to hide.

It's not that I want to be hidden, per se, it's more that I want to be invisible. I don't want to be here but I can't be anywhere else.

Hospitals have always made me very uncomfortable. I'm not sure that there's anyone out there who really loves them, especially when they are visiting a loved one, but I'm not sure everyone feels exactly like I do.

I pace in front of the vending machine

like a tiger in a cage. I'm not angry or impatient, rather resigned to my fate.

Perhaps I'm in a daze.

Owen has undergone surgery, but he is still in critical condition. They had to put him into a medically induced coma and now it's just a matter of waiting.

The doctors don't have any answers. Doctors, plural. There are five of them. One is the spokesperson, the others are part of her team, whatever that means.

But at least what we are getting is the combined opinion of all of them put together. They said that as if it's a good thing.

How does that saying go again? A camel is a horse that was designed by a committee. Committees aren't always what you want.

Whether or not it's something I want now, I have no idea.

I have no idea how to feel about anything. In fact, I feel nothing.

In one of the magazines in the waiting room, they have an article about how autistic children can't tell emotions. The teachers who work with them use a chart and point to different emotions to help them identify how they feel.

Smiley face for happy.

Sad face for sad.

The article is old and I wonder if they just rely on emojis now. Anyway, if you asked me how I feel right at this moment, I would've pointed to the sad face.

Two minutes ago, I would've pointed to the angry orange face and the inward pointing eyebrows.

Over the last few days, my mom and Nicholas have taken turns trying to tell me to calm down.

If there is one thing that I have been throughout all of this it is calm.

Stoic, some would say.

Dead on the inside, someone else would say.

Mom was here during the surgery but ever since then she hasn't been around much. According to her, there is no point to us sitting in the waiting room when we can wait just as effectively (or ineffectively) at home.

If his condition changes then they'll call us, she reassured me. But I read online that it's important to talk to coma patients, that it helps them remember who they are after they wake up so I make a promise to myself to wait for it to happen.

It's Wednesday and I haven't seen her a bit and I don't expect her to show up today either. But she surprises me.

"Want to get a cigarette with me?" she asks, waltzing over.

I don't smoke but I say sure.

The sliding doors open for us and we step outside into the falling light. It has been days since I have had a fresh breath of air and I breathe in deeply.

"You called and asked me about this woman who Owen is in love with," Mom says, taking a drag of her cigarette.

I had left her a message about it yesterday. The doctor told me that it's nice for the patient to hear voices of people who care about him.

So, I thought I would try to find her, wherever she is, and ask her to come visit.

"Do you know who she is?" I ask even though I know that it's a long shot.

Owen wasn't the type to tell that many people things that mattered to him and our mother would probably be at the bottom of the list anyway. But he did spend some time with her and, who knows, maybe something slipped out.

She finishes one cigarette and lights another. I wait but she doesn't say anything. Still, I can feel that there's something on the tip of her tongue.

"What did he tell you?" I ask.

Again, she doesn't reply.

If she had nothing to say then she wouldn't be here.

She wouldn't have brought it up.

"I don't know how to tell you this, Olive, but I guess I'll just come right out and say it."

"Yes, please do."

She picks at her peeling nail polish on her thumb with the index finger of her other hand.

Finally, she puts out her cigarette and says, "It's you."

My tongue touches the roof of my mouth and my mouth drops open.

"But he's...my..."

"No, he's not," she cuts me off before I finish the thought.

I touch my collarbone with my hand.

"I didn't want to tell you but, hell, now is as good a time as ever, I guess," she says, lighting another cigarette.

"I adopted you when you were a kid. I'm not your biological mother and your dad is not your biological father. That's probably a good thing, huh?" She laughs a loud raspy laugh that originates somewhere in the pit of her stomach.

My world tilts on its axis and I start to fall.

I take a step to the side to catch myself only to realize that I wasn't falling at all.

I start a few different questions at the same time without really knowing where I am going

"So... I don't... *what* are you saying exactly?"

"Owen knows that you're not his sister. He has known since you were about fifteen. And then in prison when you started writing him and you two really got to know each other...he fell in love with you. Hard."

"No, you're lying," I say, shaking my head.

"I have lied about a lot of things, Olive, but I'm not lying about this."

I touch the bun at the back of my head and stick the flyaway strands of hair back into it.

"Why would he tell you this?" I ask, shaking my head.

"Because we got high together and things like this tend to come out when you have expanded your consciousness a bit. Besides, he has always been my little boy. He has always come to me with everything, not like you."

I don't know how true it is or how much of this is just a figment of her imagination.

But I do know that people tend to say a lot and reveal a lot of secrets when they've had a bit too much to drink or smoke.

"So, what am I supposed to do with this now?" I ask.

My blood pressure rises with every passing minute until my head feels like it's going to explode.

"I don't know," she says. Leaning back, she bends her knee and props her foot up against the wall. "I guess do what you were going to get this girl you found to do... talk to him. Remind him that there's someone out there who loves him. Maybe he'll come back to us."

After my mom leaves, I wander the grounds of the hospital for about forty-five minutes.

I don't know what to think about this. I don't know if she's lying or why she would if she were.

She has lied about a lot less and about a lot more important things but this one really feels like it's out of left field.

And what if she is telling the truth? What then?

There's a small rose garden where I find a seat. I've never thought of Owen as anything but a brother and that's no different now.

Except of course, it is. Knowing how he feels about me and the possibility that it's true makes me... angry. The rage roiling in the pit of my stomach surprises me.

I don't know how to process anything of what she has said.

She's not really my mother, so who is?

Owen isn't my real brother, do I even have one?

They are both family, but are they?

And then there's the other small but not at all inconsequential detail; Owen is in love with me.

When I asked whether this woman he cared about had a husband and a family and a boyfriend he said no. But still he couldn't tell her how he felt.

Now, I know why; she's actually his sister. Or has been for twenty-odd years.

Man, my family is fucked up.

If I had smoked, I'd be reaching for a cigarette right now.

Instead, I take out a piece of gum and

pop it into my mouth. I make a giant bubble, filling it with as much air as it can fit and blowing in a little more until it bursts over my face.

"Oh, there you are!" Nicholas says, standing by the gate to the garden. "I've been looking for you everywhere. You weren't answering your phone."

I give him a little nod as I try to peel the gum off my face. I look at him but I'm really staring somewhere past him.

There's a large oak tree that the wrought iron fence wraps around and a little black bird is sitting on one of the lower branches.

"How's Owen?" Nicholas asks, coming over and giving me a peck on the cheek.

"The same."

"I'm sorry, but I think we should just wait and see. It's going to be alright, Olive."

"Yeah, I hope so," I mumble, watching the bird take a few hops and then fly away.

"Hey, listen." He nudges me. "Have you heard from Sydney?"

When I don't respond, he adds, "You know, your roommate?" As if I would've forgotten who she was.

"No, not recently."

"Well, you're not going to believe this," Nicholas says. "Sydney's back."

\*\*\*

Thank you for reading TELL ME TO STAY!

I hope you enjoyed continuing Nicholas and Olive's story. Can't wait to find out what happens next?

**One-click Tell Me to Run Now!**

 From the moment we met, Nicholas Crawford has been an enigma.

He's a man with an unknown past and a mysterious future.

HE'S A CRIMINAL, **a liar, a mastermind and the love of my life.**

.   .   .

I BECAME A CRIMINAL FOR HIM.

I rescued him.

Now it's his turn to do something for me.

WHEN I DISCOVER that everything I believed about my family is a lie, I need his help to uncover the truth.

WHO AM I ?

Where do I come from?

Why is there so much deceit?

I'M in a dark place and I'm all alone.

He is the only person who can pull me out of it.

He is my only hope, what happens if that's not enough?

.   .   .

*DECADENT and delicious 4th book of the new and addictive Tell Me series by bestselling author Charlotte Byrd.*

**One-click Tell Me to Run Now!**

---

SIGN up for my **newsletter** to find out when I have new books!

You can also join my Facebook group, **Charlotte Byrd's Reader Club**, for exclusive giveaways and sneak peaks of future books.

I appreciate you sharing my books and telling your friends about them. Reviews help readers find my books! Please leave a review on your favorite site.

# CONNECT WITH CHARLOTTE BYRD

Sign up for my **newsletter** to find out when I have new books!

You can also join my Facebook group, **Charlotte Byrd's Reader Club**, for exclusive giveaways and sneak peaks of future books.

I appreciate you sharing my books and telling your friends about them. Reviews help readers find my books! Please leave a review on your favorite site.

Tangled up in Pain

Tangled up in Lace

Tangled up in Hate

Tangled up in Love

**Black Series**

Black Edge

Black Rules

Black Bounds

Black Contract

Black Limit

**Lavish Trilogy**

Lavish Lies

Lavish Betrayal

Lavish Obsession

**Standalone Novels**

Debt

Offer

Unknown

Dressing Mr. Dalton

# ABOUT CHARLOTTE BYRD

Charlotte Byrd is the bestselling author of many contemporary romance novels. She lives in Southern California with her husband, son, and a crazy toy Australian Shepherd. She loves books, hot weather and crystal blue waters.

Write her here:
charlotte@charlotte-byrd.com
Check out her books here:
www.charlotte-byrd.com
Connect with her here:
www.facebook.com/charlottebyrdbooks
Instagram: @charlottebyrdbooks
Twitter: @ByrdAuthor
Facebook Group: Charlotte Byrd's Reader Club
Newsletter